MERLIN'S KIN

Other August House books
by Josepha Sherman

• *A Sampler of Jewish-American Folklore*
(American Folklore Series)

• *Rachel the Clever and Other Jewish Folktales*

• *Once Upon a Galaxy: The Ancient Stories that Inspired Star
Wars, Superman, and Other Popular Fantasies*

• *Greasy Grimy Gopher Guts:
The Subversive Folklore of Childhood*
(with T.K.F. Weisskopf)

• *Trickster Tales:
Forty Folk Stories from Around the World*

•

August House Publishers, Inc.
P.O. Box 3223
Little Rock, AR 72203-3223
1-800-284-8784 (order line)
order@augusthouse.com

MERLIN'S KIN

WORLD TALES OF THE HEROIC MAGICIAN

Josepha Sherman

August House Publishers, Inc.
LITTLE ROCK

Published 1998 by August House, Inc.,
P.O. Box 3223, Little Rock, Arkansas, 72203,
501-372-5450.

Printed in the United States of America

10 9 8 7 6 5 4 3 2 1

LIBRARY OF CONGRESS CATALOGING-IN-PUBLICATION DATA

Sherman, Josepha.
Meriin's kin : world tales of the hero magician / retold by Josepha Sherman.
    p.   cm.
    ISBN 0-87483-532-2 (hardcover)
    ISBN 0-87483-519-4 (trade paper)
    1. Tales. 2. Magic in literature. 3. Title.
    GR73.S47   1998
    398.21—dc21   98-24524

Executive editor: Liz Parkhurst
Project editor: Sarah Scott
Cover design: Susan Shankin

AUGUST HOUSE, INC.   PUBLISHERS   LITTLE ROCK

Contents

Introduction

𝔐erlin: man of mystery, wielder of wondrous powers, kingmaker and prophet. His tale is forever linked with that of King Arthur and the knights of the Round Table, with the entire mythos of Camelot, familiar to all of us in English-speaking lands. Merlin: the strange, almost eerie magician who stands just to one side of the rest of humanity.

Yet Merlin is not alone of his kind. He has kin in every corner of the world. For magicians are found among all peoples, all cultures, and some of those magicians' tales can be found in this book. There are dark names among folklore's pages: Faust, Circe, Medea, and those other sorcerers who seem to exist to plague the magickless folkloric hero. Yet none of them have been included in this book. To gain admission here, each magic-wielder must have displayed heroic deeds, a desire to do some good, and a refusal to use his or her powers for harm.

But why are there so many tales of magicians in the world's folklore? Why does the very word "magic" send a thrill both of fear and delight through us? Perhaps because the world can be a difficult, confusing, perilous place. No matter how sophisticated we may be (or believe we may be), no matter how far we think we are from "old superstitions," all of us still harbor, deep within us, the longing to change things with a wave of a hand, or perhaps a Word of Power.

Not every culture approves of magicians. Sometimes fear of the unknown, of the outsider who just doesn't fit in, turns magic from a neutral gift into something dark and demonic, which denies the magician a heroic role. But tales of magic, no matter what sort, cut across political boundaries and through walls of culture: Every society, approve of magicians or not, still likes to hear stories about them.

This book includes both the traditional magician familiar to us from medieval tales, the one whose power may come from books of spells or even demons, and the shaman, who is priest and healer as well as wizard, and who generally gains his or her gifts from the world of spirits. The two classes often overlap; a Hungarian *taltos*, a magical person possessing great powers, may transform himself to living fire like a shaman, while a Siberian shaman's animal-spirit helper sounds very much like the familiar spirit of a magician. The one constant in these tales is magic.

One theme that runs through many of the folktales of world magicians is that of a learned man, one who is often an historical character, who is also a priest or minister. How could such a man become linked with tales of the "forbidden" arts? For many centuries, unfortunately, there has been a distrust or even downright fear of the learned, often equating the Black Arts of sorcery with any sort of study at all. Since the clergy in European societies were often the only ones in a community to be educated, it was an easy jump of illogic to assume that the priestly course of study included the Black Arts. The height of such illogical assumptions came, perhaps, during the eleventh century. Pope Sylvester II happened to be an intellectual interested in the sciences— and was, therefore, supposed to have sold his soul to the Devil! But this linking of magic with a learned or religious person is not a new thing, nor can it be blamed on any one religion or culture; the Egyptians of the first millennium BCE were already assuming that Prince Khaemwaset, a priest, was also a magician.

We can't feel too superior. While we, in America at least, don't usually accuse intellectuals of being in league with evil, the mistrust of education is, alas, still very much with us. Phrases such as "cultural elite" are bandied about, and we cling to the unflattering picture of an intelligent person as an "egghead" or "nerd" who is, for all his knowledge, seen as inferior; we stereotype scientists as "mad." And we all can and indeed should read about the witch hunt in Puritan Salem—and the witch hunt in modern McCarthy-era America. No, we certainly can't feel too superior.

The magician will always be with us. It's up to us to determine how to view that magician: as a figure of terror to be shunned or denied, or as an invitation to study the unknown, which can be wonderful rather than terrible; in the process of studying the magician, we will, hopefully, learn a little more about ourselves and what it means to be human.

Welcome to the world of the hero-magicians.

The Lord of Pengerswick

A Magician from Cornwall

His name is not known to us. But even though the tales speak of him only as the lord of his estate, as the Lord of Pengerswick, none of them deny that he was a powerful mage, indeed—and that he used his magic only for good.

The same, alas, was not true of his father, the first Lord of Pengerswick. That lord was a powerful magician, but one who practiced some very Black Arts. There was never a scrap of kindness to him, nor any idea of using his powers to help others. Why, he thought, should he aid those too weak to take care of themselves?

This cold-hearted first Lord of Pengerswick had a colleague in sorcery, and that was the Witch of Fraddam, a woman who had long ago sold her soul to the devil and never regretted it. She was every bit as foul and evil as the Lord of Pengerswick, and skilled in every type of poison as well.

After some years, the sorcerer had a son. His wife died in the birthing, but that cruel man never shed a tear for her. Ah no, his attention was all for the baby. For right from the start, it was clear that the small scrap of a child had inherited every bit of his magic.

The Witch of Fraddam was delighted. "Isn't this splendid?" she crowed. "Another who'll become as skilled in the Black Arts as we! Another to turn to Darkness."

The baby grew to be a boy, and the boy to be a young man. But all this while, no matter how his father praised or threatened him, he refused to turn to Darkness.

"The boy has too strong a will," the Witch of Fraddam muttered. "He will be a danger to us."

"He will," the old Lord of Pengerswick agreed. "Sad to be rid of my son and heir—but I am not yet too old to get myself another."

And so he wed again, this time to a shallow, self-centered woman who cared nothing about her lord's sorcery. In his castle also was Bitha, the niece of the Witch of Fraddam. Bitha was as nasty and shallow a creature as could be. She had taken a fancy to the lord's son. And so, alas, had the lord's new wife. But when he, too wise to be ensnared in such perilous matters, would have none of either of them, Bitha whispered in the wife's ear. And she, the lord's second wife, cried out to the lord that his son had assaulted her.

"Here's my excuse to be rid of the boy," the old Lord of Pengerswick muttered to the Witch of Fraddam.

"Oh, indeed, indeed," she growled. "Sell him into slavery. They'll beat the magic out of him. Or maybe even kill him."

Neither of that evil pair knew that the youngster was listening. "If I stay here, I'm doomed. I don't yet know enough magic to fight them both."

So that night the young man fled his father's castle, hiding his tracks by the magic he did know. And no one, not his father, not the Witch of Fraddam, could puzzle out where he'd gone or what he was doing. The two of them, disappointed over losing such a prize, took to quarreling. So terribly did they fight that at last the Witch of Fraddam poisoned the old Lord of Pengerswick and vanished into the night.

Years passed. One day, long after the old lord's death, the young Lord of Pengerswick returned, and returned with a lovely bride, dark of hair and slanted of eye, at his side. He had been living all these years in the Orient, where he had met this young woman, his equal in magic. Together, the young people studied their craft, and while they studied, they fell in love.

So here was a Lord of Pengerswick living in the castle once again, and with him his mysterious wife. Soon enough, the people of Pengerswick learned that their new lord was an even greater magician than the old. He was a mysterious man who allowed no strangers in his castle, and all the servants were sworn by magic vows to tell nothing of their master's affairs. But every now and again, the villagers below the castle heard the magician's voice chanting some great and wondrous spell, or heard his magical wife's harp playing soft and intricate music. Sometimes the chanting and the music together wove powerful charms, magics that flashed like wildfire. The people would nervously cross themselves at such uncanny sounds and sights.

But they weren't really afraid, or at least not *too* afraid. For everyone quickly learned that the new Lord of Pengerswick used his powers only for good. No crops failed in that land, no plague attacked. And as for the Witch of Fraddam, who had poisoned the old lord, she still did her best to work evil, but the Lord of Pengerswick continually foiled her strongest spells.

"I must be rid of him," she snarled. "I *will* be rid of him!"

Everyone knew that the Lord of Pengerswick rode down from his castle on a great black mare. No one else could ride that mare, but the horse moved as softly as a lady's jennet for him. Some folk whispered that it wasn't a horse at all, but a wild-eyed devil that the magician had defeated in battle and captured in this form. But the Witch only laughed at that. "This is a mare, born of a mare, nothing more than that."

However, upon considering this mere horse, an idea flashed to her mind, and she set a trap. Out of the depths of her knowledge, the Witch of Fraddam concocted a poison so terrible that it could slay a living creature at a touch. She poured it very carefully into a large cask, which she placed right where the Lord of Pengerswick was sure to ride.

"I'll frighten the mare. She'll shy and dump her rider right into the poison. He'll shrivel, he'll wither, he'll burn to ash. And I'll be rid of him!"

Sure enough, the Lord of Pengerswick came along, riding his fine black mare. And just as intended, the mare shied—but the Lord of Pengerswick was well aware of the trap because his magic screamed a warning to him. He steadied the mare and whispered magical words in her ears. The mare then whirled and kicked out with both heels, sending the large cask flying, and all the poison spilled harmlessly out. Before the Witch of Fraddam could flee, the cask came crashing down on her. Next, the Lord of Pengerswick shouted out a command, and the cask became a boat whereby the devil, riding a great whirlwind, seized it, and the Witch of Fraddam trapped within it, and dumped it into the sea. So there it stays, and there she rides, and there, a prisoner of the sea, she remains.

And, the Lord of Pengerswick, feasting his eyes on his magic and wit, observed, "She is settled till the day of doom," and rode for home.

Gwydion

A Magician from Wales

Gwydion came from a magical family. His uncle, Math, son of Mathonwy and ruler of the land of Gwynedd—which we now know as northern Wales—was a powerful magician; indeed, he was the strongest in all the realm. But young Gwydion was no weak conjurer. In fact, he could transform sticks to boars, weeds to shoes, whatever he wished into whatever he wished, himself included, without any difficulty at all. And, since he was a good man at heart, his great talent was generally no problem to himself or others. Generally, that is.

Gwydion had gotten himself into trouble because he felt sympathy for his love-sick brother. He had used his magic to win a young woman for his brother—but she had been the ritual foot-holder for Math, a divine whose power was such that his feet were never to touch the bare earth. So, the young magician had spent time in animal shape as a result of that affair, thanks to his angry uncle's greater magic.

But the young woman and Gwydion's brother were meant to be together, so now another foot-holder must be found. This was no easy matter, since the young woman chosen must be pure of heart and body. Aranhrod, Gwydion's sister, came forward (though, truth to tell, they had little enough to do with each other, she like chill winter, he like bright summer) to claim the title. Gwydion wondered at that, since he knew his sister was hardly pure in either sense. But come forward she did.

Any candidate for foot-holder must first step over a magic wand, and the moment Aranhrod did, she cried out and gave birth on the spot to two children. One, a finely formed boy, was named Dylan, son of the wave (for, as it turned out later, he was a child of the Fair Folk of the sea). The second was barely formed at all, a baby boy too soon torn from the womb. Aranhrod fled without a backward glance, but Gwydion, heart aching with pity for his too-new nephew, swept the poor thing up in his cloak and rushed off for his quarters. There, he conjured a chest into a warming container, as close to a womb as his magic could make it, and placed the baby safely within.

"Live, little one," he whispered. "Grow strong and healthy."

And the baby did. Taken at last from the chest, he was as healthy and lusty-lunged as any normal baby. Gwydion soon found a wet nurse for him, a cheerful woman with milk for more than her own baby. However, the one thing Gwydion could not do for his nephew was name him. That task, by law and magic, must be done by the boy's mother.

"In time," Gwydion said. "In time."

And time passed. The unnamed baby grew to a fine, handsome boy, fair as Gwydion and warm of heart.

"Now, what woman would not be joyous to see so fine a son?" Gwydion thought, watching the boy laughing and running at play. "Even Aranhrod surely will feel her cold heart warm at the sight of him."

But Aranhrod, when Gwydion confronted her in her palace, had no desire to be reminded of her humiliation back at Math's court. "That is not my son. I place this curse on him: He shall have no name save from my lips, and my lips shall never utter a name for him."

The magic in the curse was strong, for Aranhrod had inherited some of the family powers as well. Gwydion drew back in horror, for how could a man without a name ever win honor for himself? "You are a wicked woman to harm one who never harmed you! But I vow that name him you shall."

Back Gwydion went to Caer Dathl, his fortress, and thought long and hard on what he must do. Then he walked along the beach below the fortress, now and again staring across the water at Caer Aranhrod, his sister's island fortress, and gathered dulse and seaweed. From this, he conjured a ship and a great mass of the finest cordovan leather. He cast magic over himself and his nephew as well, making them look like nothing more than a common shoemaker and his apprentice, then set sail for Caer Aranhrod to visit his sister, Aranhrod. A messenger came scurrying down from the fortress to see who had come, then went scurrying back up to his mistress.

"A shoemaker has come here, lady, and he has the finest leather that ever I've seen."

Aranhrod had her feet outlined on a bit of cowhide. "Give this to the shoemaker. Have him make me a pair of shoes."

But Gwydion cleverly made them far too big. The next pair he made too small. Then he grumbled, as a real shoemaker might, "I cannot work from charts alone! I must work from the lady's living foot."

Aranhrod was not about to let a stranger into her fortress. She went down to him. And while Gwydion was pretending to measure her foot, the boy, her son, played at hunting. A wren landed on the boat's mast, and the boy shot it down with a stone from his sling so neatly that Aranhrod cried out, "What a sure hand that fair-haired child has shown!"

"And what a fine name you have given him!" Gwydion cried, dropping his magical disguise. "Lleu Llaw Gyffes, Fair-haired Sure of Hand, shall he be!"

Raging, Aranhrod shouted, "I put this curse on him: he shall never take arms till I arm him—and that, I shall never do!"

For a man in the warrior-world of Gwynedd not to be able to use weapons was a harsh curse, indeed. "A wicked woman you were, a wicked woman you are," Gwydion told her. "But I swear this: he shall take arms!"

He sailed back to his fortress with his newly named nephew, soothing the boy's fear. "You have a name. I will win you arms, never fear. Have I not given my word?"

But first some time had to pass, time in which Lleu Llaw Gyffes grew to a fine youth just on the edge of manhood. But Gwydion saw the pain in Lleu's eyes when the other boys his age practiced with sword or spear.

"Come," he said to his nephew. "Time for you to be armed."

He cast a spell over them both, making them look like a world-weary bard and his apprentice, then travelled back to Caer Aranhrod. Bards were always welcome in those days, so it was with no difficulty at all that Gwydion and Lleu won entry. Gwydion happened to be a fine teller of tales, so Aranhrod listened to him without the slightest doubt that he was, indeed, a bard. Furthermore, as a bard, he and his "apprentice" were given a fine sleeping chamber that night.

But long before dawn, Gwydion arose and called upon his magic powers. As the sun rose, the air filled with the sounds of war: trumpets blared, men shouted, weapons clashed. It was not long before Aranhrod herself came to the chamber and said, "Bards, I will not deny that we're in a sorry fix. There is no way out for you, for any of us, but to fight. And we need every able-bodied man. Will you fight?"

"Gladly," Gwydion said, and began donning the armor Aranhrod's men had brought. "Och, but my lad there is still new to weaponry. Won't you help him with his armor, lady?"

Now Aranhrod was in such a frantic state, she thought nothing of it. But as she finished helping the "apprentice" don armor, the clamor of battle stopped as suddenly as though cut off by a wall. The disguise fell from Gwydion and Lleu. "Thank you, sister!" the magician cried ironically. "For now Lleu is armed, and by your own hands."

"My curse on him!" she shrilled. "May he never find a wife of any race known upon this world!"

"He has a name, no thanks to you, he bears arms, no thanks to you, and he shall yet find a wife, no thanks to you!"

But Gwydion left that fortress saddened. This time no simple trick of illusion would help. Where would Lleu find a wife if not among the races of the world?

"I fear that I cannot help Lleu," Gwydion thought, "but perhaps Math can."

So off Gwydion went to his uncle to tell his troubles. "All is not lost," Math said after a while. "Come, nephew. We must gather flowers."

"Flowers!"

"If we cannot find a bride for Lleu, then we shall make one."

Math and Gwydion worked long hours over the flowers they had gathered. What spells they said, what charms they wove none can guess. But at the end of it all, there were two very weary magicians—and one woman, new as the springtime, lovely as the flowers. They named her Blodeuedd and gave her to Lleu as his bride. Math gave to them Cantref Dinoding to rule over, and for a time all went well with Lleu and his strange lady.

But Blodeuedd was, after all, made of flowers. She lacked the deep soul of a true human woman. One day

Gronw Pebyr, Lord of Penllyn, stopped by Lleu's fortress when he was not at home. Blodeuedd gave Gronw hospitality. And after the two of them had spent some time in staring hotly at each other, she gave him a great deal more.

"But I have a husband," she murmured to Gronw.

"Such can be removed."

"Not he. He is the nephew and great-nephew of magicians, and not vulnerable as ordinary men."

Gronw retorted, "He still breathes like ordinary men. There must be a way to slay him. Find it, Blodeuedd."

That night, Lleu returned home, and Blodeuedd pretended to be joyous. But later, she pretended just as easily to be sorrowful.

"Why now, wife, what's wrong?"

"If you must know, husband, I am worrying about your death. If someone should kill you—"

"Och, foolish! It is not easy to kill me."

"Why not? Are you not a man? Love, please, please, don't jest with me!"

Lleu saw the worry in her eyes and thought—how not?—that it was all for him. "Love, hear me: It would not be easy to kill me even with a cast of a spear. For that spear could only be made by someone working on it a year, and only on each holy day at that."

"But then you could be slain!"

"Not easily. For I cannot be killed in a house nor outside, neither on horse or on foot."

"Then—then how *could* you be slain?"

He still thought the worry in her eyes was for him, all for him, and Lleu smiled at his wife and told her, "One must make a bath for me on the river bank, and construct a roof over the tub, as though to make it a good shelter. Then that one must find a goat and bring it beside the tub. I must stand with one foot on the goat's back, the other on the edge of the tub. Only then can I be slain."

Of course Blodeuedd pretended to be greatly relieved—
and of course she sent word to Gronw, who set about making
the spear. A year passed, and then, when Blodeuedd heard
that the spear was done, she said to Lleu, "This is foolish of
me, my lord, I know it. But … och, I cannot picture how one
could possibly stand with one foot on a goat's back and the
other on the edge of a tub! Surely that's impossible!"

In that year, she had given Lleu nothing but assurances
of her love. And he, young man that he was, never thought
once of how foolish he was being. "Come, love, I'll show you
how it can be done."

So he stood with one foot on the tub placed at the
riverbank and all roofed over, and the other foot on the goat.

And Gronw cast the fatal spear. Lleu screamed as it
pierced him. But Lleu had just enough magic in his blood to
change to an eagle's form and fly away.

Gwydion, far from there at the court of Math, felt his
nephew's cry in every nerve and sinew. "Uncle—"

"I felt it, too."

"I will find him," Gwydion swore. "I will know no rest
till I find him."

He wandered here and there and here again, and rested
one night in the hut of a swineherd. Gwydion, waking early,
saw one sow set off from the pen at a good clip and followed,
wondering. She came to a tree, where she fed on that which
fell from it. And that was a terrible thing: rotten flesh. Gwydion looked sharply up, and there in that tree, on the upper-
most branch, was a sickly eagle, weak and all but dead, and
it was from this bird that the rotten flesh fell.

"Lleu," Gwydion breathed. "You don't even remember
being human, poor wounded lad, do you?"

Hearing no response, he began, very softly and carefully, to sing the eagle out of the tree with his magic. At the
first verse, the eagle slid down from the upper branch to a
lower. At the second verse, the eagle slipped down to the

lowest branch. And at the third verse, he landed weakly on Gwydion's knee. Gwydion touched him with magic, and the eagle was Lleu again, but Lleu was so gravely thin and sick that Gwydion feared he would die. Hastily, the magician brought him home, and all the doctors in Gwynnedd tended him.

By the end of the year, Lleu was healthy again. "Now," Gwydion murmured to Math, "is the time for justice."

"Indeed," Math agreed, and mustered his men.

Off they rode for Cantref Dinoding, which had all this while been in the hands of Gronw Pebyr and the treacherous Blodeuedd. When Blodeuedd saw the army, she cried out in terror, "Gwydion has come for me!"

She fled out across the wilderness, but no matter how she ran, Gwydion was right behind her. At last she could go no further. "Don't kill me!" she shrieked.

"I won't," Gwydion grimly promised. "But for the shame and harm you brought upon Lleu, you shall never see the light of day again. You shall fly only by night, and all the other birds shall hate you. Yes, birds, Blodeuedd. No longer flowers, but owl, no longer Blodeuedd but Blodeuwedd." And Blodeuwedd, "flower face," she became, for that is the look of an owl's face; Blodeuedd, now in the shape of an owl, flew despairingly away.

As for Gronw Pedyr, it was Lleu who cornered that villain. "What fine will you accept?" Gronw cried. "Copper? Silver? Gold? Name your blood-price and I will pay it!"

"No blood-price save this," Lleu replied coldly, "a cast of a spear as you gave to me."

Gronw snatched up a great stone to shield himself, but so powerful was the fury of Lleu Llaw Gyffes that his spear stabbed right through the stone—and through Gronw, too.

Lleu Llaw Gyffes took possession of his land once more, and ruled it well. And as for Gwydion and his adventures after—that tale is not known.

Michael Scott

A Magician from Scotland

$\mathcal{N}$o one can say for certain how Michael Scott came by his magical powers. The tales all agree that he wasn't born with them, and that the boy and later the man travelled to many lands in search of wisdom and studied in many schools.

One of those schools, though, the tales claim, was dark, indeed. For it was none other than the infamous Black School, where the students were taught by the very forces of Darkness, and from which School one student and his soul never escaped. In the Black School, the tales claim, Michael Scott learned his lessons well in all the magical arts. But the boy found within himself a stubborn streak that would not let him study beyond a certain point. He would never, the young magician swore to himself, never cross that temptingly thin, so very perilous line into the trap that was evil magic, nor ever weaken enough to sign away his soul.

And Michael Scott escaped the Black School, body, soul and shadow intact, by running at full speed just when his demonic teacher was reaching out to snare him. The demon grabbed Michael's heavy cloak, as Michael had planned, thinking it was the boy—and so won nothing but claws full of wool.

After his narrow escape, Michael Scott travelled on through many lands, stopping in Spain and in Italy, but not yet satisfied with his learning. At last he wandered back to

Scotland, to his native Selkirk. There he met up with two other young men and travelled with them a while, walking sticks in hand and packs on backs. They came to a lonely loch, a lake. It was a wild, wild place, and Michael Scott soon felt the forces of dark magic. He told his companions, "We should not walk here. I—" But before he could finish, a terrible white serpent lurched up out of the water, lunging at him.

There wasn't time to run! Scott swung his walking stick with all his might and hit the serpent with so great a blow that he brought it crashing to the ground. Drawing his dagger, the young man sliced off the snake's head before it could recover, then stood struggling to catch his breath until his two companions, who'd run off in fright, returned.

"The night's coming on," they cried, grabbing his arms. "This is no place to linger!"

Soon they reached an inn. Michael was too worn to tell of his adventure, but his companions babbled excitedly to the innkeeper, who gave the young man wary glances. She fancied herself a mistress of the Black Arts, she did, and there was something strange, she sensed, about this young man.

"A serpent, you say?" she asked. "A white one? I'll pay well any one of you who brings me a piece of that snake."

Now, Michael was not about to oblige her, just as much aware of her pretentions toward sorcery as she was of his magical learning. But his two companions hurried off and soon returned with a good chunk of the dead serpent.

"This will make a fine stew," the innkeeper said, and laughed to see the boys' disgust. She was, she claimed, only joking, and set about giving her three lodgers fine food and a cozy bed for the night.

But Michael alone did not sleep. He tiptoed back to the kitchen and watched the innkeeper set the chunk of serpent to simmering in a pot over the fire, all the while murmuring soft chants to herself. At last she left the hearth for a moment, and the young man stole up to the pot, stuck in a wary finger, then, even more warily, licked it clean.

Ah, wonderful! Wild new wisdom raced through Michael's mind, telling him what the birds were singing, what the animals said, and how to command spirits and demons. The serpent's magic flowed directly into his brain, and now Michael Scott knew he was a true magician.

The years passed. Michael Scott still studied, still tested his wisdom, even summoned demons to do his bidding. But in all that while, he never broke the vow he had secretly sworn: he never crossed the line into evil, nor bartered away his soul.

It was a risky game he played. Sometimes, since even a magician must earn a living, he found work as an astrologer, but had to guard his tongue lest he read the stars too accurately and make folk think him a demon.

"This is too uncertain a living," he told himself, and set himself up as an architect, since that was yet another skill he'd learned along the way.

But here, too, he'd found a risky game to play. There was nothing at all wrong with Scott's designs; they were practical and elegant in one. But what he, used to the ways of magic, had forgotten was that no human workers could have completed those designs in time without going through a fortune.

"This isn't a true problem," Michael Scott claimed when his employers asked how he could ever finish a stately mansion on schedule. "The building will be completed, and completed exactly on schedule and cost not a farthing more than it should."

It did, indeed. For that night, Scott conjured up demons and bound them to his will, so they would complete the building. And of course, with workers unable to weary or grow bored, the job was done before the sun rose. Delighted and awed in one, Michael's employers put other business his way.

And yet, there comes a limit to how many houses and walls and bridges a town may need. The demons worked and worked and never stopped, refusing to be banished. For Michael had made a mistake. When he had conjured them, he'd been in such haste to get the job completed that he'd never told the demons how or when his summoning would end.

"That means I've placed myself and probably all Selkirk in peril! If I can't find a new job for the demons, one that will keep them forever busy, they'll certainly attack me, body and soul, and maybe go after all the town as well."

But Michael never flinched. He knew that some where in his mind was the answer. And sure enough, he found it before the demons could attack. "Go," the magician commanded them, "and spin me ropes by which I may climb to the back of the Moon. But I order you thus: Those ropes must be spun only of the sea's sand."

Off the demons flew to the seashore. And there, since demons are not at all clever beings, they still sit, endlessly trying to spin ropes from sand.

After that narrow escape, Michael was a bit more cautious in his magic, continuing to walk the narrow line between Good and Evil. So wary was he that when the folk of Scotland needed to know when Shrovetide would fall that year—that being the holy day that set the calendar for all the other holy days of the year—they went to Michael Scott for help.

"It's already Candlemas," they cried. "There is almost no time in which to reach Rome and return."

"There is more than enough time," Michael assured them.

Alone, he conjured up a spirit. "How swift are you?"

"Swift as the wind," the spirit claimed.

"Not swift enough," Michael said, and banished it, summoning another. "How swift are you?"

"Swifter than the wind and the wind before that wind."

"Still not swift enough," Michael said, and banished it. This time he worked a mighty spell, just this side of Darkness, and conjured up none other than the devil. Did Michael's heart quail at the sight of the terrible dark thing he'd summoned? If it did, no fear showed in his voice as he asked, "How swift are you?"

"Swifter than thought," came the contemptuous reply.

"You'll do," Michael said, forcing even more contempt into his voice. "I command you by all the Holy Names to take the shape of a horse. Nor may you shift from that shape till I release you."

It was a powerful spell indeed, one that almost drained Michael's strength. But there the devil stood in the form of a coal-black steed. Michael mounted, and the demon horse launched itself into the air, speeding across the sky.

Now of course the devil was furious about being used like this, and in being forced to speed to holy Rome at that, and plotted to destroy his rider. As they flew over the sea, the devil asked suddenly, "What do people cry when in distress at sea?"

The devil hoped that Michael would utter Holy Names, which of course no demon could endure—and which would give the devil a perfect chance to let Michael drop and drown.

But Michael Scott was ready. "What do they cry but, 'Higher! Higher! Faster to Rome!'"

And, fuming, the devil was forced to carry Michael safely to Rome. There, the magician learned the date for Shrovetide from the Pope himself. "But you will never return to Scotland in time for it!" the Pope exclaimed.

"Oh, I shall, Your Holiness," Michael assured him gravely.

And of course, mounted on his demon-horse, he did. When Michael let the devil go, the devil muttered, "There will be a special place of pain prepared for your soul."

"But I shall never visit it," Michael said.

The years passed, and even magicians grow old. When Michael Scott knew at last that his time had come, he ordered that his body be laid out on a hill. "Wait and watch. Three ravens and three doves will fly toward my body. See which reaches it and you will know which way my soul shall travel."

And so Michael Scott's body was laid out on the hill as he had ordered. Sure enough, three ravens black as night came speeding toward the body, but they were in such haste that they flew right past it. Three doves flew to the body, and reached it before the ravens could recover.

"His soul has been saved!" the people cried.

Michael Scott had kept his vow.

Mongan

A Magician from Ireland

Though Mongan was called the son of King Fiachna of Ulster, he was actually the son of Fiachna's queen and the Otherworldly King Manannan mac Lir, whose enchanted realm lay under the sea. Fiachna's wife had lain with Manannan in exchange for Faerie protection over her husband. And that was how young Mongan was born possessing magical powers.

But merely possessing magic isn't the same as knowing how to use it. When Mongan was only three years old, Manannan took him down to the wondrous kingdom of Underwave so that the boy could learn to use his powers. It was a strange, sunless place glowing by its own light, and there were so many strange wonders for a child to see that Manannan must have been hard-put to keep his son's attention on his lessons. But Manannan, being an ageless Faerie, had endless patience. And once he was satisfied that his son knew enough magic to take care of himself, he brought Mongan back to Ireland so that the boy could learn to be human as well.

His strange schooling served Mongan well. He grew to be a fine, clever prince, comfortable both with human ways and the ways of magic. He was also most happily married to the princess to whom he'd been betrothed at birth and who was called Dubh-Lacha, the Black Duck, for her lovely hair, dark and glossy as the wing of a duck.

Unfortunately, other men hungered for Dubh-Lacha as well. And even a clever fellow like Mongan could be caught off his guard. He was visiting the King of Leinster, who owned a wonderful herd of cows, their hides shining like snow in the sunlight, their ears red as any rubies. So taken with these cows was Mongan that he forgot to hide his delight. The King of Leinster saw this and smiled to himself.

"I will give you this herd," he said graciously, "for only the smallest of goodwill tokens. A goose, perhaps, or—ha, yes, give me only one small black duck and the herd is yours."

Mongan agreed—and only then realized that the black duck the king wanted was none other than Dubh-Lacha!

"I gave my word," Mongan moaned. For that was back in the days when no man of honor ever broke a vow.

So off the King of Leinster went with Dubh-Lacha. She, however, clever lass, tricked the king into vowing not to touch a hair of her dark, shining hair for the space of a year.

"By then," she told herself, "Mongan will surely have magicked me home again."

So there was the King of Leinster with a prize he couldn't so much as touch. And there was Mongan stunned by the loss of his wife—and by the knowledge that he'd lost her through his own foolishness.

But then Mongan said, "If it was by my folly I lost Dubh-Lacha, it will be by my cunning that I win her back."

Off he went to Leinster. Along the way, Mongan saw a monk, Tibraide, trying to cross a rushing stream, and asked for his aid.

"Be off with you," Tibraide snapped. "I'll not be aiding a magician."

Magician, am I? Mongan thought. *Then magician I'll be. And it's aiding me you'll be.*

He raised up his magic wand and conjured a pretty bridge. Tibraide thought it was real and started across—only to be dumped right into the water. Mongan snatched up Tibraide's gospel book and, with a touch of his magic wand, turned himself into the perfect likeness of the monk. Off Mongan went to Leinster and read the gospel to the king, who believed this was, indeed, a holy man.

"Now," Mongan said with feigned humility, "I will hear the confession of that fair lady."

He pointed to Dubh-Lacha. The king, suspecting nothing, let Dubh-Lacha go to the "monk," and Mongan in a moment would have carried off his wife.

But, alas for trickery, Tibraide fished himself out of the stream far too swiftly and come running, dripping and panting. "Now here's a plentitude of Tibraides!" gasped the king.

"*I* am Tibraide!" the monk shrieked. "*That* is Prince Mongan!"

That broke Mongan's spell. He fled for his life.

"But I'll not give up my dear wife so easily!" he vowed. "If this transformation didn't work, then, I think, another shall."

So off Mongan went to Cuimne, the Hag of the Mill. Cuimne was a magical being, too, and though she was an ugly creature, she was no more evil than, but just as cunning as, a fox. Mongan told her his plan, and the Hag laughed and said, "A fine trick. Yes, I will help you."

So Mongan raised his magic wand over Cuimne and turned her into the perfect likeness of Princess Ibhell of the Shining Cheek, then raised his magic wand over himself and turned himself into the perfect likeness of Prince Aed the Beautiful. Off they went to the King of Leinster. The king took one look at Cuimne, disguised as Princess Ibhell, and fell madly in love.

"May I have a black duck in exchange?" Mongan, impersonating Prince Aed, asked mildly.

"Och, take what you will," the king said, never taking his eyes from "Princess Ibhell." "Leave this lovely creature with me."

Grinning, Mongan ran off with Dubh-Lacha. When he let his disguise fall, she laughed and said, "I knew it was you! But who was that princess?"

Mongan told her, and she burst into new laughter. "The poor king! I almost pity him."

So it was that the King of Leinster found himself in the arms of the Hag of the Mill, mockery ringing in his ears.

But Mongan and Dubh-Lacha lived long and happily— and Mongan never made another foolish vow.

Friar Roger Bacon

A Magician from England

Roger Bacon was born the only son of a rich farmer in England's West Country. The farmer sent his son to the local parson, thinking that the boy should have just enough learning to help him run the farm wisely.

But Bacon took to learning with wild joy. He came home and begged his father to be allowed to go on with his studies, and the parson agreed, telling the farmer that a boy this clever should not have his intelligence wasted; he would surely go on to Oxford University itself.

The farmer was furious, and perhaps more than a little jealous that his son should prove wiser than he. "You shall be no better learned than I!" he raged at Bacon. "It's not fit, it's not right. And if I hear any more of this 'learning' nonsense, you shall suffer for it!"

The boy listened in silence. Then, without a word, he turned and left the farm forever. He found learning where he could, here and there, entering a cloister for a time, where he took holy orders and became a friar. At last Friar Bacon had managed to round out his education to the point where he could, indeed, attend Oxford University. And there, perhaps, the story might have ended—but one of the arts that Friar Bacon studied at Oxford was magic.

Word of this new magician reached the king. Wondering what marvels Friar Bacon could perform, the king sent a messenger, a fine young man of gentle birth, and invited him to the royal court. Friar Bacon smiled.

"Thank the king for his kindness," he told the messenger. "But move swiftly lest I appear at court before you."

The messenger looked at him with scorn, never believing that such a mild-mannered friar could ever be a magician of even the weakest skill. "Scholars may lie as they will, but that doesn't mean I must believe them."

Friar Bacon didn't like being called a liar. "Not only will I prove my words, I will announce to the world your sweetheart's name. And I will do both within four hours."

The messenger sped off as best he could. But when he reached the royal court—why, the friar was there waiting for him.

The king, who had already been astonished by Bacon's sudden arrival, said, "We have heard many wondrous tales of you. Now, we pray you, let us see some further proof of your art."

"I will do what I may," the friar said quietly. He raised his magic wand, and instantly the court was filled with exquisite music. "This is to celebrate the Sense of Hearing."

He waved his wand again, and suddenly five comic dancers appeared, who amused the audience greatly before disappearing back into the air. "That," said Friar Bacon, "was to celebrate the Sense of Sight."

He waved his wand a third time, and before the courtiers appeared a table covered with delicious fruits of every kind. As soon as all had had their fill, the table and its contents vanished. "That," Friar Bacon told the court, "celebrated the Sense of Taste."

Next came wondrous wafts of perfume, celebrating the Sense of Smell, and last, the softest of furs and velvets, celebrating the Sense of Touch.

Friar Bacon waved his wand one more time, and the wonders were at an end. "Amazing!" the king cried. "Wonderful!"

He removed the fine golden necklace from his throat and gave it to the friar. All applauded—save one.

The messenger who had called Friar Bacon a liar glared at him, but the friar smiled. "I said that I would name your sweetheart," he said. "And so I shall."

With that, he pulled aside a heavy curtain, revealing a sweaty kitchen-maid, her ladle still in hand. As the court burst into laughter at this common wench being the fine gentleman's sweetheart, Friar Bacon took his leave.

"I never lie," he said.

But once he was back in his Oxfordshire home, the friar had a chance to use his skills for more than fantasy. A young gentleman, desperation in his eyes, came to him for help.

"I was a fool," the young man began, "a wastrel who lived only for the fun of spending coin. That is how I brought my entire estate to ruin."

"You would not be the first to make that claim," the friar murmured. "But there's more to this than a young man's dissolution."

"Ah, yes, far more. You see, I'd borrowed money from everyone who would allow it, and all my creditors howled after me for payment. Then a stranger confronted me and offered me money enough to pay off all my debts if only I'd agree to—to meet certain conditions."

"A stranger," Friar Bacon said grimly. "I can already guess his name. But go on."

"I met the stranger in a wood, as he'd insisted, and sure enough, he had sacks of gold coins with him, just as he'd promised. I would have taken them, and gladly, but the stranger held up a hand. 'First,' he said, 'we must seal our agreement. You will pay off all your debts. But once they all are paid, you will become my slave.'"

Friar Bacon winced. "And you agreed?"

"I thought nothing of it! Or rather, I thought that surely he jested, that he merely needed my services for a time. I needed that money! So—I agreed." He shuddered. "And then the stranger ... the stranger ... changed most monstrously. 'You will pay off your debts today,' he ordered me, 'and I will come for you tomorrow night.'"

"And tonight," the friar said, "is the fatal night. Well now, don't despair. Let me think the matter through. You are sure that the *exact* wording was that once you had paid off all your debts, you would become That One's slave?"

"Yes."

"Splendid! Simply splendid! No, young man, don't stare at me like that. I haven't gone mad. But I do think I see the way to free you. Now, here is what you must do ..."

That night, trembling and hopeful at the same time, the young gentleman returned to the wood. Sure enough, there was the terrible Stranger, looming like a patch of utter darkness in the night. "You have paid your debts," the Stranger hissed. "You are mine."

"N-not so fast. I say that one debt remains."

"No debt remains! I have seen to it!"

"I don't mean to argue with your, uh, majesty. Will you let a third party settle this?"

The Stranger laughed coldly. "Do what you will. You are still mine."

Just then, Friar Bacon appeared, as casually as though he had merely been out for a midnight stroll. "Good sir," the young gentleman called, "will you not settle a quarrel for us?"

"I will do what I may."

Impatiently, the Stranger summarized the situation. "He has paid his debts. He is mine."

Friar Bacon held up a hand. "Not so quickly. The terms were that he pay off *all* his debts. Yet he owes you for the kindness you've shown him. Has he repaid the loan to you?"

"No," the Stranger snarled.

"Why, then that one debt remains unsettled. And as long as he does not pay the devil any coin," the friar added, voice ringing out with magical force, "then that one debt remains unpaid. And you, oh Enemy of Mankind, cannot claim his soul. So, *begone!*"

With a great roar, the Stranger vanished, leaving only the stench of sulphur behind.

The young gentleman, as can well be imagined, mended his ways after that, and never did pay a coin, real or figurative, to the devil. And Friar Bacon went on his way.

However, his adventures were far from complete. Friar Bacon was sent to France by his king to conquer a city—one that had never surrendered to England. The king confessed to Bacon: "But I have not the arms to mount a major campaign."

"Art is needed," the friar returned, "not arms."

Off he went to France, where he studied the city's high walls for a time, then smiled. The city could be taken easily enough, and by science, not magic.

Friar Bacon had a great magnifying glass manufactured, and set it so that the sun's rays would set fire to the city's town hall but leave the massive city walls untouched. This seemingly magical attack frightened the citizens so much that they surrendered. Even though the townspeople were defeated, Friar Bacon made sure that they were all treated with courtesy. And as a result of that courtesy, he was invited to visit the court of the King of France.

The French king had a magician at court, a German conjurer named Vandermast. He was a mysterious man who had learned his craft from the devil.

Now, Vandermast had no idea that Friar Bacon was a magician. The conjurer declared that he would entertain the king, and called up a likeness of the ancient Roman warrior, Pompey. But Friar Bacon, wishing to compete with Vandermast, called up a likeness of Julius Caesar, who had beaten Pompey in life and who beat him now.

Vandermast, glaring at Friar Bacon, only now recognized him for what he was; the two magicians then began to fight a duel of illusions. First the friar conjured the likeness of the Hesperian tree with its golden apples that was so amazingly real that all the courtiers gasped at its beauty. Second Vandermast called forth the likeness of Hercules, who had, or so the Greek myth claimed, plucked the golden apples.

"Not this time," the friar said, and set his will to overcoming the other magician. Sure enough, at Friar Bacon's will, the figure of Hercules turned, scooped up the startled Vandermast, and vanished!

"Don't fear for him," the friar said. "I have but returned him safely to his home in Germany."

"I fear you've made a bitter enemy," the king replied.

But Friar Bacon merely smiled and returned to his own home in England.

Meanwhile, Vandermast had, indeed, been returned to Germany. There, furious over the insult Friar Bacon had paid him, he plotted the friar's death.

Friar Bacon, however, had seen in his books of magic that some great peril was to befall him within a week unless he could prevent it.

"I dare not sleep," the friar thought. And so he held a brass ball in one hand as he read, with a brass basin below it. Should he fall asleep and let the ball drop, the clang of metal would, he hoped, wake him.

And peril there was. Vandermast had hired an assassin, a Walloon mercenary from Flanders, to kill the friar. The assassin found Friar Bacon dozing, the brass ball still in his hand. But just as the Walloon raised his sword, the friar's hand opened enough to let the ball drop, and the clash of metal woke him.

"Who are you?" he commanded. Magic was in the words.

"I am a Walloon mercenary," the assassin told him helplessly, "hired by Vandermast to kill you."

"Do you believe in Hell?"

"I believe in nothing."

Then Friar Bacon conjured the spirits of the damned and let the Walloon see their terrible suffering. "No," the Walloon gasped, "Ah, no. No, no, no."

He fled, repented, and lived a good life from then on.

But Vandermast did not. First he heard that Friar Bacon was dead, then he learned from a fellow conjurer that Bacon was alive and well. So furious was he that he quarrelled with the conjurer. The quarrel turned to a fight, and the fight turned to true war between the two till at last the devil grew weary with their noise and took them both.

But Friar Bacon lived on as a good and gentle man. And when at last he died, full of years, the devil had no claim on him.

Virgil

A Magician from Medieval Italy

$\mathcal{S}$ ome say that Virgil was the son of a nobleman, others say nothing about his rank at all. But all the tales agree that Virgil started his life as an ordinary boy, without a trace of magic but with a quick, inquiring mind. One day, bored with his schoolwork since he had already outpaced all his teachers, he went walking in the wild hills, where he discovered a dark, mysterious cave. He plunged inside to explore.

Virgil had gone quite a way into the cave, and was beginning to wonder if he shouldn't turn back while he could still find his way out, when he heard a cold voice whispering his name.

"Virgil ... Virgil ..."

"Who is it? Who calls?"

"Look, Virgil," the voice whispered. "Do you see the round stone set in the floor?"

By now, the boy's eyes had grown accustomed to the dim light filtering in from outside through cracks in the rock. "I see it," he said warily, "and the bolt holding it in place."

"I am trapped beneath that stone. Free me, Virgil."

"Not so quickly. First, who and what are you?"

"I am a mighty spirit," the cold voice whispered, "trapped under here till Doomsday. Free me, Virgil, and I will give you books to make you the mightiest of all magicians."

That sounded intriguing to Virgil. But the boy wasn't about to act so trustingly, not when what was almost certainly an evil spirit was involved. "Not so quickly," he said. "First give me the books. Then I will free you."

The spirit ranted for a bit, but what choice was there? "The books are hidden behind rocks to your left and right," the cold voice whispered.

Sure enough, they were. A glance through them sent excitement racing through Virgil, for they were full of marvels.

But now he must free the spirit. Virgil pulled the bolt and stone aside, revealing a small opening. A great dark shape swirled up out of it, filling the cave in a moment, and the boy fell back against a rock. No doubt about what he had just released! He could feel evil whirling about that shape like a cold, cold mist.

But Virgil was ready to trick the spirit. "You lied!" he said in seeming contempt. "You are no mighty spirit at all!"

"What's this? What's this? I *am* mighty, boy! I will show you just how great my powers are!"

Virgil only yawned. "Nonsense. No mighty spirit could ever have fit through such a tiny opening."

"I did! I did!"

"Bah, I don't believe you. You are nothing but a fraud."

"Why, you foolish little worm of a boy! Watch this!"

When the evil spirit swirled back down into the opening, Virgil quickly replaced the stone, bolting it back in place. "You are the fool, spirit, not me. Stay there, you evil thing, as it was meant to be. Stay there till Doomsday!"

Virgil took the magic books and left. Alone in the hills, he hungrily began his magical studies. The days turned to months, the months to years, ten years in all. At the end of those years, even though he was still a young man, Virgil had become a true magician.

But then he received a desperate message from his widowed mother. While he'd been lost in the study of wonders, she had been slowly cheated by the rich relatives of her deceased husband. Now she was at the edge of poverty.

Virgil hurried home, abashed that with all his magic, he had never realized that his mother was in peril. "But now I shall set things right," he assured her.

At first he decided against using magic. He thought, "Surely such arts aren't needed here!" But the rich relatives merely shook their heads at his protests, claiming that they had taken no more than their just due. And when Virgil appealed to the Emperor of Rome, he received not a word of satisfaction.

"We shall," the Emperor's message read, "take the matter under advisement. It shall take years to check every record."

"The Emperor," Virgil realized, "has been getting a percentage of the stolen profits from our relatives. Well now, I can play games, too."

When the Emperor's tax collectors came the next season to claim the royal share of profits due from the new corn harvest, Virgil shrugged. "Do you see any corn?"

But he had, of course, hidden it all by magic. "Then we shall tax the profits from your wine harvest," the tax collectors decided.

Virgil shrugged. "Do you see any grapes?"

He'd hidden all that away by magic, too. No matter what the tax collectors tried to tax, Virgil had hidden it away. At last, muttering angrily, they returned to court.

"You shouldn't have made an enemy of the Emperor," Virgil's mother warned.

"He shouldn't have made an enemy of me!" the magician replied.

Sure enough, the Emperor declared Virgil a rebel, and sent soldiers to besiege his castle. But Virgil cast a mighty spell that froze the soldiers in their tracks like statues. He left them there all day as a warning. When he let them go again, the soldiers fled without a word.

"You cowards!" the Emperor raged at them. "Are you afraid of one man?"

Yes, after spending that time as statues, they certainly were! But one didn't admit such things to the Emperor. He sent a whole army after Virgil. But Virgil cast a mighty spell, creating the illusion of an icy, raging river before them and a river behind them, trapping the army on a narrow strip of land. There they stayed all day and night with no food or drink, smelling the delicious scents of roasting meat coming from the castle and hearing the sound of happy laughter.

One soldier, however, had been lagging behind and hadn't been caught by either river. He rode full-tilt for Rome and cried out to the Emperor: "Your army is trapped and starving because of Virgil's magic!"

The Emperor set out with every court magician he could find. Together, they all cast a Sleep Spell—and the spell caught Virgil off-guard. His servants fell instantly asleep, and he only managed to stay awake by fighting the spell with all his will. Mind foggy and hands feeling heavier than stone, Virgil struggled to open his magic books, slowly turning page after page to find the spell he wanted.

Yes, here it was! To battle the Sleep Spell, Virgil shouted out a fierce Word of Power. Instantly, the Sleep Spell recoiled on the court magicians, and they fell fast asleep while all of Virgil's men awoke. The illusion of the two rivers was broken and vanished—but the Emperor's soldiers and even the Emperor himself were turned into living statues. There they were, and there they stayed for a full two days.

On the morning of the third day, Virgil lifted his spell. The Emperor and his soldiers became living folk once more, and the Emperor wisely sued for peace. He repaid Virgil's mother all the money owed to her and punished the rich relatives who had cheated her.

"Will you be my Court Magician?" he asked Virgil.

Virgil knew that the Emperor feared him. Fearful men never trust those who frighten them. But at least as Court Magician, he would know more easily if another attack on him or his people was planned. "I will," he agreed. "But I will not live in your palace. That would be too dangerous for your people when I work my magical experiments."

This statement was perfectly true. The Emperor gave Virgil permission to build a fine castle for himself. It was, of course, magical, the Castle of Eggs, so named because its foundation rested on nothing more solid than eggs. Virgil also built a tower for the Emperor, one from which the Emperor could overhear any words of treason. And even if there wasn't exactly peace between Virgil and the Emperor, neither was there war.

In another matter, however, Virgil was not so successful. Magician or no, he was still human, young and romantic. Alas, his magic frightened away the young women at court, or worse, made them mock him. His anger at their mockery only made matters worse. Lonely despite all his powers, Virgil thought he would never find true love.

But one day, traveling the world by magic, he landed in a beautiful garden by moonlight, and came face to face with a young woman wandering alone. Virgil fell in love with her on the spot. And, more wonderful than any magic, she fell instantly in love with him.

"But you must not stay here!" she cried, "My father is the Sultan of Babylon, and if he finds you here, he will slay you!"

"I'm not afraid. Princess, I am Virgil the Magician. Let me show you the wonders of my castle."

To his delight, she had no fear of his magic. She gladly flew with him and wandered with him through his castle's halls and gardens; they were joyous in each others' company. But at sunrise, Virgil returned her to her father's palace.

"Will you come to me tomorrow?" the princess asked.

"I will," Virgil promised, "though all your father's guards will block my path."

Alas, a servant overheard Virgil and the Sultan's daughter and raced off to the Sultan. "Your daughter has allowed a—a sorcerer, to visit her!"

The Sultan slipped a powerful sleeping potion into some wine and left it where his daughter was sure to find it and give it to her mysterious guest. Sure enough, his plan worked. She gave the cup to Virgil and he fell into a deep, drugged sleep.

He woke to find himself in chains in prison. The princess was chained in there as well. "You have betrayed me!" the Sultan shouted at them. "You have both brought dishonor to my name!"

"I have done nothing dishonorable," Virgil protested, "and neither has your daughter. This I swear on my magic."

"The oath of a sorcerer is worthless! And the fate of a sorcerer is the stake and the flame! You shall die at sunrise."

"Then I shall die as well!" the princess cried.

"So you shall," the Sultan said coldly. "He has corrupted you with his darkness."

When dawn came, Virgil and the princess were led to the stake, which was piled high with dry wood. Virgil showed not the slightest sign of fear. He was waiting to free himself at the one moment when the guards released his chains in order to bind him to the stake—yes! For this instant, he was free!

Virgil flung up his arms and shouted out a Word of Power. Suddenly all there, all save Virgil and the princess, thought that a great flood of raging water had roared down upon them. They all began frantically trying to swim.

"Hurry," Virgil whispered to the princess, "before they realize this is only illusion. Will you come with me? Will you wed me?"

"Yes and yes," the princess told him.

The two of them then flew magically away from Babylon to Virgil's castle. There they were wed, and there they lived in joy and magic for the rest of their lives.

Csucskari

A Magician from Hungary

*I*n the long-ago days, there was no sun in the sky, no moon, no stars. People knew there were such things as the sun and the moon, but they had no idea where such wonders could be found.

In those dark days, there lived a king with a court of wise men. He sent them out, every one, to find the hero who could fix the sun and the moon in the sky, declaring that anyone, rich or poor, noble or common, who succeeded in that would have half the kingdom and the hand of his daughter as well.

Meanwhile, three young Gypsy brothers had left their home so as not to be a drain on their poor parents, and were sitting in the wood, wondering what was to become of them. The youngest was named Csucskari, and he, though no one knew it yet, was a *taltos*, a magical person possessing strange powers.

Some of the royal wise men came upon these three boys and sighed. "They're poor, ragged Gypsies. But the king did command that everyone, rich or poor, be told."

So the wise men told the three Gypsies of the king's command. Fire flashed in Csucskari's eyes. "I will set the sun and the moon in the sky," he stated.

So off the wise men and the three Gypsies went to the king. "Are you sure you can set the sun and the moon in the sky?" the king asked.

"I can," Csucskari assured him. "But first we must sign a contract: I will set the sun and the moon in the sky, and when I do, you will give to me half the kingdom and the hand of your daughter in marriage."

The king had such a contract prepared. Csucskari needed no pen. He signed with his fingernail, signed in letters of gold. Then the young *taltos* made his brothers swear that they would obey him in every regard and be astonished by nothing they saw.

They set out on their quest. As they traveled through the forest, his brothers saw only trees, and on those trees, only leaves. Csucskari read on a leaf words written in gold: He who entered this forest would meet a great boar who would try to tear him to pieces. Then he would meet a sow who held within her a box filled with twelve wasps. Any who seized the box and freed the wasps would have the power to set the sun and the moon in the sky.

Sure enough, the boar appeared. Csucskari was ready to fight, but the boar said to him, "I knew when you were smaller than the smallest grain of wheat in your mother's womb that we were destined to meet. When you meet the sow, don't kill her; take the box, but sew up the wound so that she may raise her piglets."

Csucskari caught the sow, cut her open and took the box of wasps. Then, remembering the boar's request, he sewed her back up again, and just like that, she was healed.

Csucskari came to a woman standing in the doorway of her house. "Greetings, Csucskari," she called. "I knew when you were smaller than the smallest grain of wheat in your mother's womb that you and my twelve-headed dragon-husband were destined to fight. And he will kill you!"

"Fight he may, kill he may not," Csucskari said. "What sign is there of his returning?"

"He hurls his great stone mace before him that it may crush his foes."

Sure enough, here sped the great stone mace. Csucskari turned in time to catch it and hurl it aside. He hurried to the bridge over which the twelve-headed dragon must ride, and hid underneath. As the dragon rode over the bridge, Csucskari stuck his sword blade up and made the dragon's horse stumble.

The dragon swore: "May your blood be lapped by dogs!" But then he realized, "It must be Csucskari who plays this trick on us. If I knew for sure, I would take his head."

"It is, indeed," Csucskari said, springing out from hiding. "But my head is not for your taking. A poor reward would it be for me, who is to set the sun and moon in the sky."

"Will you fight with sword or strength?" the dragon asked.

"With neither," Csucskari said. "I have no time to fight with you." With one sweep of his sword, he cut off all twelve of the dragon's heads.

On Csucskari went, and soon came to a second house. Here, too, waited a woman who warned Csucskari of her ten-headed dragon-husband, brother to the first. Once again, Csucskari hurled away the giant mace, once again hid under the bridge, once again, tripped the dragon's horse.

"This is Csucskari's doing!" the dragon cried. "He has slain my brother and now I'll slay him."

"Come, then," Csucskari said, springing out from under the bridge. "See if my life is so easy to take."

Their swords clashed again and yet again. But Csucskari ended the fight with one clean sweep that took off all ten of the dragon's heads.

Again, on Csucskari went. He came to a third house, with a third woman in the doorway waiting for her eight-headed dragon-husband, the brother of the twelve- and ten-headed dragons. "What sign does he give of his arrival?" Csucskari asked.

"None," the woman said. "Here he is now."

"So now," the dragon shouted, "you have slain my two brothers. And I shall slay you!"

"Better for you to ask what death you wish for yourself!" Csucskari said.

For three days, Csucskari and the dragon fought, first with swords, second with strength, and third with magic. On the third day, the dragon turned himself to red flame, Csucskari to green flame, but still neither could win. Csucskari was in sore distress, gasping for air. Far overhead circled an eagle crying mournfully.

"Well you may be mourning the ruin of the one who can set the sun and moon in the sky. Bring me water, eagle, and I shall give you the dragon and all his cattle. And there shall be a wonderful light in the sky."

So the eagle brought water to Csucskari, and Csucskari found new strength. He cut off the dragon's eight heads with one mighty sweep of his sword, left the eagle to feast, and went his way.

Meanwhile, the three widows who had been wed to the twelve- headed, ten-headed and eight-headed dragons, and who were sorceresses in their own right, met to plot revenge. What they didn't know was that Csucskari had taken the skin from an old cat and turned himself into a perfect copy of that cat. While in disguise he heard every word of their plan.

Csucskari rejoined his brothers, who had been sitting morosely in the forest, wondering what to do. "Are you hungry, brothers?" the *taltos* asked, and raised a commanding arm. Instantly a table spread with food and drink appeared, and all three brothers feasted. "Never fear," Csucskari told them. "I have found the means to set the sun and moon in the sky. But till I do that setting, we must be on our guard."

They headed off toward the king's palace. But the first sorceress, she who had been the wife of the twelve-headed dragon, began to burn at their backs, rousing fierce hunger within them. There ahead of them lay a wonderfully golden loaf of bread.

"Don't worry, brothers," Csucskari said, "I will deal with this." He snatched up the loaf and made the holy sign over it. Blood ran from the loaf—and that was the end of the first sorceress.

Now the brothers were tormented by the fiercest thirst. Ahead stood a well, but Csucskari blocked his brothers' path. "Don't worry, brothers, I will deal with this." He made a holy sign over the water. It ran red with blood—and that was the end of the second sorceress.

Then the brothers saw the most wondrous pear tree, heavy with ripe fruit. They longed for it, but Csucskari reached it first. "Don't worry, brothers, I will deal with this." He made a holy sign over the fruit. Blood ran from the tree—and that was the end of the third sorceress.

But the mother of the three dragons, an old hag with an iron nose, came speeding up faster than thought, riding a shovel through the air. This, Csucskari thought, was something with which he could *not* deal!

"Run, brothers! Run for that smithy."

The smith gave them shelter. But he was a strange man with savage strength. When he grew angry, he would tie a hundred knots into a tiny mannikin. Csucskari thought uneasily that if the smith could do that to a tiny mannikin, he could surely tie two hundred knots in a *taltos!*

"I will help you," the smith said. "But you must stay here to serve me."

What choice did the brothers have? That monstrous iron-nosed hag was close behind them.

"Very well!" Csucskari cried. "Only stop the hag."

The smith did that with alarming ease, by simply throwing a cauldron of melted lead at her. Now Csucskari was even more sure that this smith could be a danger since he was a man with such fierce temper and such great strength—perhaps magical strength. And here, since the smith had helped them, Csuckari and his brothers had to serve him.

But the smith also had a wife. Csucskari set about to charm her, and charm her he did. He persuaded her to ask her husband where he got his marvelous strength.

At first the smith didn't want to answer. Then he grudgingly told her, "It's my shirt of mail that I never remove. Without it, I am just an ordinary man."

That night, the smith's wife slipped the mail shirt off him while he slept and gave it to Csucskari, who tried it out by tying one of his brothers into over three hundred knots. Well now, it worked! Quickly, he untied his brother and woke up the smith.

"We've changed our minds," Csucskari told him. "We're leaving your service, now."

When the smith tried to stop him, Csucskari tied him into over three hundred knots.

"Don't leave me like this!" the smith said. "I agree, you're free to leave."

Csucskari untied him, gave him back his mail shirt, and left with his brothers. They were nearly back to the king's palace.

"Wait, brothers," Csucskari told them. "Before I set the sun and moon in the sky, I really must take a nap."

A *taltos* has no need of sleep. Csucskari was merely testing his brothers. But they, of course, didn't know that. The eldest brother waited until Csucskari began to snore, then took out his razor. The middle brother cried, "What are you doing? You already shaved!"

"It's Csucskari I mean to shave," the eldest brother snarled. "I mean to cut his throat! Then the half a kingdom and the princess will be mine!"

"You can't do this!" the middle brother said. "It was Csucskari who went through all the trouble, Csucskari who fought all the fights. Besides, he's our brother! Csucskari, wake up!"

"I am awake," Csucskari told him, getting to his feet. "I was testing you both. You, middle brother, pass the test, and I thank you. But you," he addressed the eldest brother, "are no longer one of us. I disown you for your treachery."

"As do I," the middle brother said sadly.

Csucskari and his brother went on their way, and he who had been the eldest of the three was seen by them no more. Soon they had reached the king's palace. Csucskari told the king cheerfully, "We have returned victorious. I don't wish the half a kingdom or the hand of your daughter; a *taltos* does not need such things. So kindly give them to my brother."

"That is as it may be," the king said. "First honor our agreement."

"Easily," Csucskari said. He released the wasps from their box. They fled up into the sky and suddenly the sun and moon were fixed in the sky. The world was flooded with wonderful light.

And the celebrating, ah, the celebrating continued for all of seven years!

Eirik

A Magician from Iceland

When Eirik's tale began, he was just another student at the Cathedral School at Skalholt. Meanwhile, a bitter old man, a heathen set in the ancient ways, had died, telling the Bishop on no uncertain terms that his prize possession, a mysterious book, *must* be buried with him. The Bishop, possibly humoring the old man, or just as possibly thinking that such a mysterious volume was better off buried, agreed.

But Eirik did not. He had overheard the conversation between the old man and the Bishop, and at the mention of the book, a spark seemed to shoot through him. It must be his; he knew that without any doubt. So off Eirik went to the graveyard, together with two fellow students, Bogi and Magnus. How they had learned the spell, no one can say, but the three youngsters managed to raise the ghost of the bitter old man, who appeared clutching his book. Nor was he about to give it up, not for soft words, not for hard blows. But at last the three boys managed to snatch away the book. The ghost reluctantly vanished, and they hurried back to the Cathedral School with their prize—which, as Eirik had known without knowing how he knew, was a powerful book of magic. All three studied, but it was Eirik for whom the book seemed to have been written. He learned every spell locked within, save one only.

"I shall use them only for working good," he vowed, and the book seemed to like that, lying peacefully under his touch.

The boys grew to manhood. Bogi and Magnus were ordained, and left Skalholt. Eirik, too, was ordained, and given his parish. But before he left, the Bishop called the young priest to him. And the Bishop was holding the magic book.

"Do you know what is written on these pages?" he asked sternly.

Eirik's heart must have quailed, but he answered calmly, "I don't know a single sign in there."

Which was true enough, for he knew them all, save that one stubborn spell. The Bishop sighed and gave Eirik his blessing, and Eirik left—after hiding the book among his belongings.

For many long years he served his community as priest. But everyone knew that if they had need of good magic, they could turn to Eirik for that, as well.

And one night a young farmer came to Eirik's house. Eirik met him at the door, saying, "Your wife, your bride of seven days, has vanished."

"Y-yes, but how did you—"

"I'd be a poor excuse for a magician if I didn't know! But as to where your wife may be ... she isn't drowned, that much I can tell you without consulting my book. But as to where else ... that," Eirik said firmly, "we shall learn."

For three days and nights, Eirik studied his book, consulting each and every spell. On the third night, he nodded. "Come," he said to the farmer and lead him out into the desolate night, amid the great crags and broken landscape. Eirik walked till he had found one rock that seemed to be what he wanted. Placing the book open upon it—the farmer noticed that the leaves lay as still as an obedient hound—Eirik began to circle the rock, chanting softly. As he did, misty figures began to form, standing huddled together in the night.

"These are mortals who live in the world of the trolls," Eirik told the farmer. "Is your bride among them? No? Ah well, then we shall just have to try again."

He thanked the ghostly figures, who faded away, then began a different chant. Again, figures formed, again, the farmer sadly shook his head. Again, the figures were allowed to vanish.

"This is no easy thing," Eirik confessed wearily. "I am rapidly running out of possibilities for—wait, now. There are still two trolls who were not included in my spells. Let us try them."

He murmured a new spell. And suddenly two trolls were there in the human realm, ugly, angry creatures who looked less friendly than the rocks around them. They carried a small glass cage. And within that cage stood the tiny, perfect figure of a woman. The farmer gasped. "My wife! That is my wife!"

"Shameful trolls!" Eirik scolded. "Creatures of darkness, let her go."

"We will not!" the trolls growled.

"Oh, I think that you will." Eirik began to shout out strong Words of Power, and light glinted about him, growing brighter with each Word. The trolls shrank back, snarling, then suddenly fled back to their own sunless world, leaving the glass cage shattered behind them. Eirik carefully picked away the bits of glass.

"There you are, my dear, quite safe."

"But she's so small!" the farmer cried.

Eirik was already chanting the spell that restored her to a normal human-sized woman running into her husband's happy embrace.

"Thank you!" the farmer cried. "Thank you!"

But Eirik shook his head. "That was a bit too easy. I will come with you, if I may, just in case."

He stayed with the couple on their farm, refusing to stay indoors. Instead, Eirik slept across the threshold, his magic book as his pillow. Sure enough, on the third night, the trolls came prowling about the farm, seeking to recapture their prize. Eirik sprang to his feet, book in his arms, and shouted out a Word so sharp and pure that the night turned as bright as noon and the sky blazed with light. The trolls screamed in fright and ran for their lives.

"They will not dare set foot on this farm again," Eirik said with satisfaction, and settled back down to sleep, smiling.

Vainamoinen

A Magician from Finland

Vainamoinen was the son not of a mortal woman but of an Air Spirit, Ilmatar. Ilmatar, impregnated by the wind, came to rest on the Earth's ocean for long years while the world formed about her and her son grew in her womb. For sixty years Vainamoinen lived and grew in that warm, safe prison, but at last could stand this strange captivity no longer and burst free into the world.

His long time in the womb had marked him. Vainamoinen was no babe, no young boy. He was a grey-bearded man, old yet not old, wise with more than human knowledge, and a skilled singer of magic songs.

But the world into which he'd arrived was still barren and bleak. Vainamoinen set about sowing the world for humankind, fruit and field and forest, and sang the world's first magic sowing song as he did, ensuring fertile crops forever after. Now the world was complete and humans flourished like the forest trees. Word of Vainamoinen's primal deeds and magic songs spread. But whenever there is one well-known for a skill, along a younger one will come to challenge him. Joukahaimen was a young magician, a spell-singer who fancied himself quite a master of the craft. He wished, full of pride and the arrogance of the untried, to pick fights with other wizards, and to sing them into defeat.

His father forbade it. His mother pleaded, "They will bewitch you, they will destroy you, and sing you into this helpless winter snow!"

"I will sing the best singer into the worst!" Joukahaimen proclaimed. Heedless to his parents' concern, he set out.

It was Vainamoinen who Joukahaimen truly wished to meet and defeat, and indeed it was Vainamoinen he met, though quite by accident. The winter snow was heavy, leaving only a narrow road down which he drove his sleigh, just as Vainamoinen was driving the other way. Vainamoinen had the right of way, but Joukahaimen refused to give it. Shaft tangled with shaft, trace with trace, and the two sleighs came to a sudden rough stop.

"Who are you?" Vainamoinen shouted. "What clan, rude one?"

"I am Joukahaimen. Now name your own lowly clan!"

"I am Vainamoinen. Move aside, youngster. I have no quarrel with a boy."

"My youth is a small matter!" Joukahaimen retorted. "It's our knowledge that's the point, our magic skill. It's he who is the master who should have the right of way."

"What do I know?" Vanamoinen said with great sarcasm. "I have always lived my life as a farmer, sowing crops. And what, young man, do you know?"

Joukahaimen never heard the sarcasm, never saw how he was being baited. He boasted of the wondrous things he'd seen and heard, expecting this old grey-beard to cringe in fright. He told of knowing the trees in every forest, the fish in every stream. He told of knowing how the North plowed with a reindeer, the South with a mare. But all Vainamoinen said was, "Childish knowledge. Easy things. What else do you know?"

Stung, Joukahaimen boasted of more wondrous things he'd learned. He told of knowing the origin of birds, the language of snakes, the heart of water from a mountain, the heart of fire from the lightning, and the heart of rust in iron. Vainamoinen heard him out, all these young man's boastings, then asked mildly, "Is this all? Has your ranting come at last to its end?"

Still not seeing how the old man baited him, Joukahaimen boasted wildly, claiming that he had plowed the sea, set the land in place, sowed it with seed, even that he'd guided the sun and moon and set the stars in the sky.

"Now I know you lie," Vanamoinen said. "No one saw you plow the sea, nor were you there when the world was made. Small wit, yours, if you claim such things."

"If I have small wit," Joukahaimen snapped, "then I'll let my sword speak for me!"

Vanamoinen only looked at him with scorn. "I'm not afraid of you, youngster, nor of your sword or wit. Enough of this game. Be off with you."

Joukahaimen nearly roared with rage. "Whoever fears to fight a duel, him will I sing into the shape of a pig! A dead pig in a dunghill!"

Vainamoinen hissed in sudden fury. That this mere child should dare insult him thus! He began to sing, began to sing the magic songs. No children's rhymes were these, no boyish things. Pure magic were they, so mighty that the land around him shook and mountains trembled.

And he sang magic over young Joukahaimen, sang green sprouts onto his bow, willows onto his sleigh's shafts, sang the sleigh itself into a pond and the horse into a rock, sang Joukahaimen's sword into lightning, his arrows into hawks, sang Joukahaimen's cap into a cloud, his gloves into lilies in the pond, and his coat into a patch of sky.

And still Vainamoinen sang, his fury yet unbated, sang against Joukahaimen himself, sang the young man into the ground to his ankles, his knees, his armpits. All the while Joukahaimen tried his best to fight back, to sing a spell-song in self-defense, but not a word would come. He could not pull so much as a foot free from the earth, and all the while Vainamoinen was singing him deeper, ever deeper!

"Wait! Good, kind, wise Vainamoinen, wait. Reverse your spells, release me. I—I will give you any payment you desire, any ransom you name."

That pierced the cloud of Vainamoinen's wrath, though it did not dissolve it utterly. "What payment would you make?"

"I have two fine bows—"

"I have no need of your bows." And he sang Joukahaimen deeper into the earth.

"I have two swift boats—"

"I have no need of your boats." And he sang Joukahaimen deeper into the earth.

"Horses, then! I have fine stallions, mighty steeds—"

"I have no need of horses." And he sang Joukahaimen deeper yet into the earth.

On and on Joukahaimen ranted, offering anything that was his to give and many things that were not. But Vainamoinen was not moved. At last, despairing, buried to his chin and spitting out mud, the young man pleaded, "Reverse your spells. Sing them backwards and release me, oh wondrous wizard. In my mother's house there lives my sister, fairest Aino. Sing me free, Vainamoinen, and she shall be your wife."

Vainamoinen paused. A wife. He had been lonely, alone of his kind. A wife would warm his days and nights. Vainamoinen sang the young man free, restoring clothes and weapons, sleigh and horse. Joukahaimen stammered out nervous thanks, no longer the arrogant young wizard, and hurried home in such haste that he crashed the sleigh against the side of his parents' house.

And so ended the duel. But alas, when Joukahaimen told his sister that she was to wed the ancient, mighty wizard, Aino would hear nothing of "mighty" or "wizard." She listened to no word about how kindly Vainamoinen would treat her, how easy and happy her life would be. No, Aino heard only "ancient." Crying that she would not be married off to an old man, and one who was not even truly human, Aino cast herself into the sea and was transformed into a fish.

Vainamoinen grieved for her, and in the grieving maybe wept a bit for himself, so old, so wise, yet so lonely. Aino stayed in the ocean and there Vainamoinen was forced to leave her.

Aino's tale ends in the sea. But Vainamoinen, the mighty wizard, went on to more adventures.

But never did he, the greatest of spell-singers, the wisest of heroes, win a wife for himself.

Mindia

A Magician from the Georgian Nation

Mindia was born a perfectly ordinary boy, to the mountain people known as the Khevsurs. All about his village towered the massive grey peaks of the Caucasus Mountains, snow-crowned even in the brief summer, and Mindia grew up as surefooted as a goat.

Yet it was that surefootedness that took Mindia from his ordinary life. Hunting in the mountains, the boy wandered into the territory claimed by the Kajis, a tribe of mountain demons.

"A slave!" they crowed, and seized him. The boy struggled, but his strength was nothing next to that of the demons. They dragged him into their gloomy lair. And there Mindia stayed.

And there, like it or not, Mindia continued to stay. The slow years passed while he slaved away for the Kajis, twelve years in all, with never a chance for escape. In these twelve years, the boy became a man—a man hungering for his freedom. Many times in those twelve years, he had tried for that escape, but if there was a way out of this gloomy place, it was a route that a magickless human couldn't find.

"Magickless," Mindia mused. "There's the problem."

The demons, he knew, renewed their powers now and then with a special meal. But a meal of *what?* Mindia had never been permitted to learn that secret. Still, in the twelve years that the Kajis had held him, they had grown used to him, to his comings and goings; indeed, now they practically ignored him. And so the Kajis didn't notice Mindia stealing silently into the cavern where they ate, where they sat around a great cauldron full of ...

"Snake meat!" Mindia realized with a silent gasp. "That's their secret magical food!"

He waited until all the demons had staggered off to sleep, then crept up to the cauldron. Was it empty? Had the demons eaten every scrap?

No! One small, slimy chunk of meat remained. Mindia fished it out of the cauldron, wincing at the feel of it and, trying not to think about what he was doing, ate every bit of the slimy meat. He waited, eyes shut ...

All at once a wild, wondrous surge of joy swept through Mindia. "It's as though I was blind and now can see," he gasped, "as though I was deaf and now can hear—I can hear *everything!*"

Worms were murmuring about digging through the earth. Roots were murmuring about drinking up water. Even rocks were murmuring slow, deep thoughts of ancient mountains.

Aie, but the demons were returning! Mindia listened to a snake, one that was determined not to be eaten, and heard it whisper about a pathway out of the caverns, a pathway back to the sunlight. Mindia crawled up and up through the narrow tunnel, squirming after the snake and praying that he wouldn't get stuck. One last mighty heave and—

Yes! He was back in the human world of mountains and valleys and wonderful, wonderful sunlight!

For a long time, Mindia stood breathing in the free air and listening to the happy songs of the birds, understanding every one, listening to the trees, understanding their rustlings. Wonderful, wonderful, he was a part of the whole world of nature!

But the demons might be following! Shaken out of his happy reverie, Mindia scrambled down one mountain, up another, on and on till at last he had reached the village he'd left that day twelve years ago.

"I am here!" he cried. "I am Mindia, and I've come home!"

The villagers stared at him warily, and some of them had their hands on swords or daggers.

"They don't recognize you," barked a hound.

"They don't believe you," hissed a cat.

"I *am* Mindia," he insisted. "I've been a slave for twelve years, but now I've escaped."

"From whom?" a man asked coldly.

"From the Kajis—"

"Demons! How do we know you're not their spy? How do we know *you're* not a demon?"

But Mindia held up a hasty hand. He was listening to something else, something the far-off forest was whispering. "Hear to me, all of you! I don't care whether you believe I'm who I claim, but you must believe this: Enemies are marching on our village, raiders from another tribe. Wait, wait, hear me out. They are still so far away that we can take them by surprise. But we must act now!"

The villagers argued back and forth, louder, louder yet. But at last they decided to believe Mindia.

"If you're lying to us," they warned, "we shall kill you!"

Mindia wasn't lying. There really was an enemy, a rival tribe marching on the village. But the villagers attacked first. Mindia fought as well, but with his magical powers. At his command, the trees dropped branches on the enemy and birds pecked at enemy eyes.

"Sorcery!" the invaders cried. "We can't fight sorcery!"

They turned and fled.

The villagers voted Mindia their leader. They all lived happily together for years, and Mindia often spoke with bird and beast and listened to what news the trees whispered.

But, alas, Mindia began to ignore his powers. Instead, he settled down, took a wife, and raised a family. Mindia became just another villager, and as he became more human, his powers waned. At last he was no more than an ordinary man.

But, happy with his wife and children, maybe Mindia didn't mind that loss very much at all.

King Solomon

A Magician from Ancient Israel

King Solomon, ruler of the land of Israel, was the wisest of men, ruler of humankind and master of spirits and demons. He was a pious man, and had determined to build a temple to the glory of God. But the king remembered the holy words that said no altar may be built of hewn stone. For stone is hewn by iron, symbolic of the sword, and the touch of war metal on a building of peace would be sure desecration.

Then how could a temple be built? Solomon the Wise pondered this problem, and at last found a solution: the Shamir. This creature, the diamond insect, was tiny but incredibly strong, and it could surely hew stones and split mighty trees for the temple's walls and roof beams.

But where was the Shamir to be found? The king, alone in his chambers, held out his hand that bore a signet ring engraved with the Holy Name. No sooner had he proclaimed that Name than a demon appeared, kneeling before King Solomon. "What is your will, oh wisest of kings?"

King Solomon gestured to the demon to stand. "I command you to tell me where the Shamir may be found."

But the demon only trembled. "Mighty king, don't be angry. I am your servant; I do not wish to disobey. But I don't have an answer for you. Only our own king, Ashmodai, has the knowledge you seek."

"And where," the king asked sternly, "is Ashmodai, King of Demons, to be found?"

"Far from here, mighty king, far from the homes of men. His palace stands on the top of a towering mountain. In that mountain as well is a wonderful well, guarded jealously by Ashmodai. When he is not at home, he closes the opening to that well with a great rock, sealing it with the touch of his signet ring. Whenever Ashmodai returns, he first examines the seal on the rock to be sure no one has tampered with it, then drinks of the pure water and seals the well anew."

Solomon the Wise dismissed the demon, then summoned Benaiah son of Jebodiah, the captain of the royal guard. "I wish you to capture Ashmodai, King of Demons, and bring him to me."

The king gave Benaiah a golden chain inscribed with the Holy Name and a sack of the strongest wine, and lent him his royal signet ring as well. Off the brave warrior went, travelling through the desert waste, climbing the harsh, terrifying height of Ashmodai's mountain, fearing nothing since he bore King Solomon's signet ring with the Holy Name upon it.

Ashmodai was not at home. Benaiah located the well, blocked with the rock and sealed with Ashmodai's seal. He didn't try to move the massive rock; rather, he simply bore a small hole through it. Through that hole, Benaiah poured the whole sackful of strong wine.

When Ashmodai returned, tall and terrible and fiery of eyes, he went straight for the well. Never noticing the tiny hole in the rock, he removed it and drank deeply. Demons are unfamiliar with wine, and very soon Ashmodai was sound asleep. Benaiah crept forward and bound the demon in the golden chain, then waited.

At last Ashmodai yawned and woke, and found himself bound. He fought to free himself, but no demon could break a chain marked with the Holy Name.

"Come," Benaiah said, "we are going to King Solomon, he who is your master."

Ashmodai gave no argument. But strange incidents happened along the way. Once he saw a happy bridal party and began to weep.

"Monster!" Benaiah cried. "Why do you weep at the happiness of others?"

"I weep because I see the future: the groom will be dead within three days."

They went on, and Ashmodai overheard a man insisting that the bootmaker make him shoes to last at least seven years. He burst into laughter.

"Why do you laugh?" Benaiah asked.

"That foolish man will not live seven days longer, yet he wishes shoes that will outlive him by seven years!"

Benaiah, sharply reminded that his companion was, after all, a demon, said nothing.

Many other strange events befell them, but at last Ashmodai stood before King Solomon. The demon shivered at the sight of the ruler of all spirits and demons, then threw down a long staff before the king.

Solomon never flinched. "What does this mean?"

"With all your majesty, mighty king, after your death you will own no more space in the earth than is measured by that staff. Yet you would rule not just your own kind but spirits and demons as well!"

"Control your anger," Solomon said mildly. "I seek only the smallest of services from you. I wish to build a temple to the Glory of God—ah yes, demon, tremble at that—and need to find the Shamir."

"I have it not!"

"Gently, Ashmodai. Who does?"

"Mighty king, it was the Shamir that was used to carve the two tablets borne by Moses. But since that day, the Shamir has been in the care of the Prince of the Sea, who has placed it under the guardianship of the woodcock. The woodcock lives in its nest on a mountain peak, and keeps the Shamir ever with it, tucked under one wing."

"So be it," the king said. "You shall bide here, Ashmodai, till the temple is built."

He summoned Benaiah. "I have a second task for you, brave captain. You must find the Shamir in the nest of the woodcock of the mountain peak, and bring it back with you. Take this with you."

He gave Benaiah a sturdy, lead-lined box and a thick pane of glass and told him how to use them. Off Benaiah went to the mountain, hunting till he found the woodcock's nest high on a rocky crag. The woodcock was away, but there in the nest, as Solomon in his wisdom had known there would be, were several of the bird's fledglings. Benaiah quickly covered the nest and the fledglings with the thick pane of glass, then hid and waited for the woodcock to return.

Here came the bird, eager to return to its young. It saw its fledglings trapped underneath the glass and began to shriek, flapping its wings, and beating the glass with its beak. But the glass would not break. The fledglings remained trapped. At last the woodcock took the Shamir, the diamond insect, out from under its wing. The moment that the Shamir touched the glass, the glass fell apart into two pieces.

"Oh, wonderful!" cried Benaiah and leaped out of hiding. He quickly slipped the Shamir into the lead-lined box and returned all that long way to King Solomon.

And so it was that with the help of the Shamir, the magical diamond insect, the holy temple was built. As soon as it was completed, Solomon the Wise released Ashmodai as he'd promised. As for the Shamir—the moment that the temple was finished, the Shamir vanished, and to this day no one has seen it again.

Volka

A Magician from Russia

Volka was born a prince, back in the days when there was no such thing as a united Russia, and Prince Vladimir ruled the various lands from golden Kiev. But Volka showed signs of what he would become, which was something more than a prince, right from his birth, when he spoke to his mother from the cradle.

"Don't bind me in swaddling clothes!" the baby told her firmly. "I must be free to roam about."

Volka was born wise. By the age of five, he could already read the most difficult of texts and write as well as any man. By the age of six, he knew every tree in the forest and every bird in the sky. And by the age of ten, Volka was already a master of magic who could transform himself into bird or beast or fish at will.

Since Volka had been born into a noble household, heir to his father's realm, he was trained in ruling and weaponry as well as in the magic that came so naturally to him. By the age of fifteen, the young magician-prince had already gathered together his *druzhina*, the traditional princely bodyguard of warriors. Since the land was at peace just then, the prince and his band spent most of their time hunting.

The winter came, and the land grew cold. "Come," Volka cried to his men, "let us hunt fine fox and sable so we may wear warm caftans in the winter cold."

The *druzhina* set their snares, set their traps, but caught not even a mouse.

"For shame, my brave hunters!" Volka laughed. He turned himself into a great grey wolf and chased foxes and sleek-furred sables into the nets. That winter, all the band went warmly clad.

The springtime came, and the land grew rich. "Come," Volka cried to his men, "let us hunt the fat ducks and geese so that we may feast."

The *druzhina* set their nets, drew their bows, but caught not even a sparrow.

"What's this, my hunters?" Volka laughed. "Empty-handed again?" He turned himself into a pure white falcon and soared up into the sky. There he caught ducks and swans and geese, enough to feed all his *druzhina*.

But one day Volka's magic told him that there was a worse foe to face than foxes, a more perilous opponent to fight than geese. He hastily assembled his *druzhina* and told them, "Sultan Beketovitch is planning to attack Rus. Ours is the nearest land to his; it is for us to stop him. Who among you will slip into the enemy camp and learn his plans?"

Terrible were the stories about Sultan Beketovitch. The *druzhina* fell silent, all those brave men staring at the ground and flushing with embarrassment at their own fear.

"No one?" Volka snapped. "Are you all such cowards? Then *I* shall go!"

Without another word to them, he turned into a great-horned bull whose first leap covered a *verst*—a league—and whose second leap took him out of sight. He reached the sultan's lands, which were guarded by a high wall and heavy metal gates, and became a little gray sparrow that flew easily over the wall and landed lightly on the sultan's very windowsill.

There was Sultan Beketovitch pacing back and forth, saying to his wife, "I shall attack Rus, I shall seize nine cities and rule in golden Kiev. The nine cities shall I give to my sons, and to you shall I give a splendid sable coat such as Empresses wear."

"Akh, no, my husband," she pleaded, "do not invade. I dreamed a black raven fought a white falcon—and the white falcon slew the raven and scattered its feathers to the wind. That falcon was the magician-prince Volka, and the raven was you, my lord. Do not attack Rus, I pray you. You will never rule in Kiev."

"I *will* attack," the sultan snarled, "and I *will rule in Kiev!*"

Will you, now? Volka thought.

Swiftly he turned from a sparrow to a marten, long and narrow and sharp of teeth. He slipped through the narrowest of holes into the sultan's armory and bit through every bowstring, gnawed through every arrow, and chewed the hilts off every sword.

Now let us see you attack Rus! Volka thought.

He became a falcon once more and flew with all his speed back to his *druzhina.* "Take arms, my warriors. We ride against Sultan Beketovitch *now!*"

They reached the sultan's lands. But how could the *druzhina* get over that high wall? How could they get past those heavy metal gates? Volka thought, then grinned and turned them and all their horses to ants—ants that could crawl easily under the gates. Once within the sultan's lands, they became men again and charged the sultan's guards. But those guards had no weapons, not an arrow, not a sword, and they turned and fled.

"We cannot stop now!" Volka cried. "We must put an end to the sultan himself."

Volka raced to the sultan's palace, to where Sultan Beketovitch hid behind doors of iron. Volka cast them open with a mighty kick, and there the sultan cowered.

"You will never attack Rus," Volka cried, "nor rule in Kiev."

He leaped at the sultan. Honorably fighting hand to hand, he used no magic at all since the sultan had none. But Volka needed no magic. He fought for the freedom of his land, and with one mighty heave, Volka hurled Sultan Beketovitch from his palace to the cruel stones below.

Such was the end of the sultan. And such was the victory of Prince Volka the magician.

Meng Luling or Ma Liang

One or Two Magicians from Han China

As befits a magical artist, no one is quite sure about this one's name! Some tales call him Meng Luling, others claim he should be called Ma Liang. They also don't agree on his age or how he gained his talents. Whatever his name might have been, he was a true magician with his brush.

Tale One: Meng Luling

Meng Luling was a quiet man, an artist who lived in a peaceful country village and spent his days happily painting the world about him. No grand visions for Meng Luling! He took pleasure in portraying ordinary, everyday events, and in showing the beauty in them.

When the magic began, it came after Meng Luling had painted two cows, and painted them so truly that they seemed ready to step right off the paper.

"If only they could! There are poor folks in the region who would love to have two fine, fat cows like these."

Did some Heavenly Power hear him? Or was the magic in him already, just waiting to be brought to life? For the cows did, indeed, come to life, stepping out into the real world. And from that day on, Meng Luling could paint magic whenever he wished. And what he wished was to help people. He painted candles for those who needed light and meals for those who needed food, and took great pleasure in seeing the happiness he brought to life about him.

But of course such a secret as magic can't be kept for long. A rich landowner heard of Meng Luling and his paintings.

"I will pay you gold and silver. And you will paint your magic only for me!"

"I paint for myself and my friends," Meng Luling said quietly. "I paint for those who need my art. I do *not* paint for riches."

The landowner couldn't accept such an answer. Maybe, he thought, the magic lay in Meng Luling's painting box. Maybe he didn't need the artist at all! So he sent his men to steal the painting box.

"What's this? What's this? There are nothing but ugly little paintings in here! A broken bowl—bah, and a—a centipede—these things are useless!"

Angrily the landowner had the paintings burned. But shortly thereafter, a farmer found that he could predict the weather. A scrap of a painting had landed in his yard, and on it was the centipede, crawling about on an ear of millet. When the weather was to be fine, the centipede stayed on top of the ear, but when the weather was going to turn foul, the centipede hid under the ear.

"The paintings were magical after all!" the landowner cried.

Angrily he sent his guards to Meng Luling. "What, again?" the artist sighed. "Very well. I've painted two works just for your master."

The landowner was surprised and delighted to receive not one but two magic paintings. Warily, he unwrapped the first, and saw a scene of a quiet pond. But as the landowner stared, wondering what magic it possessed, the painted waters stirred. Out hopped a toad, then another, then another. Soon his entire estate was full of toads!

"Burn the painting!" the landowner cried. "Quickly, quickly!"

The toads disappeared with the painting. Wiping his brow, the landowner nervously unwrapped the second painting. It looked innocent enough, a scene of a child fanning the fire in a stove. But as the child fanned, smoke billowed out of the painting, filling the landowner's house, sending him coughing out into the courtyard.

"Look! Look! The roof's on fire! My house is burning!"

At least the painting burned up with it, and the fire vanished. But half of the landowner's house stood in ruins.

"I'll kill him! I'll kill Meng Luling!"

But as the landowner and his guards came running to kill him, Meng Luling looked up from his painting with a tranquil smile. "I've been expecting you. But now, I fear, I must say goodbye."

The painting was of a cloud sailing across a peaceful sky. Meng Luling stepped onto it. The cloud soared up with Meng Luling riding it as calmly as though he sat in a fine boat. As the landowner shouted and shook his fist in helpless rage, Meng Luling sailed smoothly away.

Tale Two: Ma Liang

Ma Liang was an orphan, a poor boy who struggled just to survive, doing hard work no one else wanted to do, but who secretly ached to be an artist. He had no money to buy even a brush and no master artist would teach a penniless student. But that didn't stop Ma Liang from learning all by himself. Nature was his teacher and twigs were his brushes. He worked as hard as ever, carrying loads for folks, bundling firewood, and cutting weeds. But whenever he could snatch a few moments, Ma Liang practiced his art. Sometimes the boy drew sketches in the sand, and sometimes he found a bit of charcoal and drew pictures on rocks. His birds seemed about to take light, his fish to wriggle off into the water. But none of the pictures lasted very long.

"If only I had a real brush!" Ma Liang thought. "If only I could afford real paint and paper!"

One night, so weary after a day of hard work that he'd fallen asleep on the floor of his little hut, Ma Liang had a wondrous dream. An old man, his beard long and smoothly white, handed him a paintbrush and told him sternly, "This is a magic brush. Use it wisely."

He vanished, and Ma Liang woke—to find himself clutching a paintbrush. Hardly daring to believe what had just happened, he started to sketch a bird and cried aloud to see color appear even though he had no paint on the brush. He concentrated on painting the bird correctly and the bird took to its wings and flew away.

"Magic!" Ma Liang cried. "The brush *is* magic!"

He began painting things for the other poor people in town, such as bucket, a candle, and a fine meal for everyone who'd ever been kind. Soon he was painting for whomever needed help.

But such wonders couldn't be kept a secret forever. The local landowner heard of Ma Liang and his magic, and commanded the boy, "You will paint only for *me!*"

Ma Liang refused. "You are a cruel-hearted man. I don't paint for cruel people."

"Then starve, fool!" the landowner roared, and had Ma Liang locked in a stable. It was a cold winter day, and the boy, the landowner thought, had neither food nor fire. Ma Liang would beg him to be allowed to paint for him!

But Ma Liang never said a word. When the landowner went to see how the boy was doing, Ma Liang grinned at him. The boy had painted a good meal for himself and was sitting comfortably before a painted fire.

"You—you—" the landowner sputtered. But he was too angry to speak. Instead, he shouted to his guards to come and take away Ma Liang's paintbrush.

But that gave Ma Liang time to paint himself a ladder and climb out of the stable. By the time the guards came running, the boy had painted himself a swift horse and was gone.

Ma Liang settled in another village. There, he painted very carefully, never quite finishing a picture so that it could never come to magical life. He made a nice living this way.

"And I am safe from greedy people!"

But at last he made a mistake and finished a painting of a crane. It came to life, soaring up into the sky. The whole village saw it and shouted out in wonder. Word of Ma Liang's magic flew as swiftly as the crane, straight to the court of the emperor.

"I must have this boy's magic for myself!" the emperor cried. He had his soldiers carry off Ma Liang to the royal palace.

"Now, boy, you will paint only for me!" the emperor commanded. "Paint me a dragon!"

Ma Liang was frightened, but also very angry. So he painted not a dragon, but a toad, a great, ugly toad. When the emperor commanded that he paint a phoenix, Ma Liang painted a skinny, smelly chicken. Furious, the emperor snatched away Ma Liang's brush and had the boy thrown into prison.

"Now I will work my own magic!" the emperor cried.

But the magic brush wouldn't paint for him. Fuming, the emperor had Ma Liang brought before him and forced himself to smile at the boy. "I had no right to threaten you, Ma Liang, or treat you like a criminal. If you will be my court painter and magician, I will give you riches. I will even give you my daughter to wed."

Ma Liang knew that this was all a lie. But he smiled and pretended to agree. "What would you have me paint?" he asked.

The emperor thought carefully. "If the boy paints a mountain," he said to himself, "it might collapse on me. If he paints a forest, wild beasts may attack me."

Ah, he had it! "Paint the sea. Yes, that's it. Paint me the sea."

So Ma Liang painted a pretty seascape, tranquil as clear glass. He then painted golden fish swimming in that sea. So beautiful were the images that the emperor said, "A boat! Paint me a boat so I may see those fish more closely."

Ma Liang painted a fine golden boat, fit for an emperor and all his court. Everyone crowded on board. Ma Liang painted a few strokes, and a wind sprang up. He painted more wind, and yet more wind! The sea surged up into wild waves, and yet Ma Liang painted still more wind!

"Stop!" the emperor cried. "Stop!"

But Ma Liang pretended not to hear his shouts. Ma Liang went on drawing a stormy sea, a stormy sky, a stormy world, until at last the boat capsized and sank. By the time everyone escaped out of the painting, Ma Liang was gone. And he was never seen again. However, some do say Ma Liang still roams the world, painting his magic for anyone in need.

Teteke

A Magician from Manchuria

Teteke looked at first glance like any other young woman, an ordinary person to be barely noted. But she possessed a shaman's true powers.

There was an official named Baldu Bayan who was no longer young, as was true of his wife as well. The one wish of both their hearts was for a child. One day their prayers were answered—they were granted a son. They named him Sergudai Fiyanggo, "fiyanggo" meaning "the last," since his mother knew she could not have any further children.

Sergudai grew and thrived and was the joy of his parents. But one day, while the boy was hunting with his friends, he said suddenly, "I need to return home. I'm not well."

Before he could say much else, Sergudai Fiyanggo fell dead. When word reached his parents, his mother fainted and his father wept. An old man appeared from nowhere and said to Baldu Bayan, "Are you going to let your son go and not even try to bring him back? Will you not even summon one shaman?"

"What good will that do?" Baldu Bayan asked bitterly. "There are at least four shamans in our village, and not one of them is good for anything."

"There is one shaman who is not a fraud," the old man said. "Her name is Teteke. She lives on the banks of the Nisihai River and is called the Nisan Shaman. Her powers are genuine and great. If any can bring back your son, it is she."

Saying this, the old man sat on a cloud, and was wafted away. Wild with sudden hope at this sight of supernatural favor, Baldu Bayan rode in haste for the Nisihai River. He passed a young woman hanging up her laundry, and asked, "Can you tell me where the shaman Teteke, the Nisan Shaman, lives?"

The young woman smiled at him. "She lives on the west bank of the river."

Baldu Bayan spurred his horse across the river, hunting for the shaman. An old man directed him to a certain house where an old woman sat. This wise-looking old one surely must be the shaman!

But the old woman only laughed. "I am no shaman. That title belongs to my daughter-in-law."

It was none other than the young woman he had seen on the far side of the river just a short time ago! "Forgive my trickery," she said, "but I have only newly come into my powers, and I was not sure I could help."

"You can," Baldu Bayan pleaded. "You must."

So desperately did he ask that Teteke sighed. "Very well. I will attempt a divination."

She began to chant, her voice high and sweet. She described the birth and life and death of Baldu Bayan's son, her information perfect in every detail. But then she stiffened and continued:

"Ihmun Han heard him. Lord of the Underworld, he sent a demon to seize the boy's soul, carry it away."

The shaman gasped, shuddered, grabbed a stick of incense, inhaled, and was suddenly herself again. "Have I divined truly?"

"You have!" Baldu Bayan cried. "But can my son's soul be found? Can he be restored?"

The Nisan Shaman asked, "Is there not a dog in your house born on the same day as your son?"

"Yes! But—"

"And is there not a three-year-old rooster and a good amount of bean paste and bundles of money-paper?"

"There is, indeed! Truly, you are a most wonderful shaman!"

"I am but young and new to my powers," she insisted as she had before. "And a journey to the Underworld is no simple thing." She had a secret she would not tell Baldu Bayan; Teteke had been both married and widowed at a very young age, and she did not wish to meet her husband in the Underworld.

But a shaman did not dare doubt her powers. Nari Fiyangoo, the old man who had guided Baldu Bayan to the right house, beat the drum for her. Teteke tied on her shaman's bells and put the nine-bird cap firmly on her head. She began to sway to the gentle beat of the drum and to the rhythm of her chant.

Suddenly her body fell as her spirit went free. The old man placed it carefully in a comfortable position, then tied up the dog and rooster by her side and placed the bean paste and bundles of paper beside her. He then continued beating the shaman's drum slowly and steadily.

Meanwhile, Teteke had reached the outskirts of the Underworld, and walked with the dog and rooster at her side while carrying the bean paste and paper. All about her, animal-spirits ran, bird-spirits flew, snake-spirits slithered.

She came to the bank of a wide river. There was a strange being punting a boat, a ferry, and the Nisan Shaman called to him, chanting out her need:

Hobage yebage If you take me across,
Hobage yebage I will give you bean paste
Hobage yebage If you take me swiftly across,
Hobage yebage I will give you goods.

The boatman heard. He was half a man in appearance, one eye, one ear, one foot, and rowed half a boat with half an oar. But he rowed her safely across. Teteke gave him three lumps of bean paste and three bundles of paper and went on her way.

But soon she came to another river, one with no ferry and no ferryman. The Nisan shaman called out to the Lord of the River:

Eikuli yekuli Young lord
Eikuli yekuli I need to cross this river.
Eikuli yekuli All the spirits
Eikuki yekuli ferry me across.

The Lord of the River let her pass; the spirits carried her across. Teteke left them three lumps of bean paste and three bundles of paper and went on.

Now she had reached the main gate to the Underworld where two *hutu*, two demons named Iron and Blood, stood guard. They shrieked: "Who dares approach? State your business!"

"I am the Nisan Shaman," Teteke said, "and I am hunting Monggoldai Nakcu."

"Then enter," the *hutu* said. "But you must leave a fee."

So Teteke left them three lumps of bean paste and three bundles of paper and entered the Underworld. She stood at the gate of Monggoldai Nakcu himself, the demon who had carried off the boy's soul, and chanted in her lovely voice with her shaman bells ringing boldly:

Hoge yage Monggoldai Nakcu
Hoge yage come forth quickly!

Her chant brought Monggoldai Nakcu out from the gates, laughing at the courage of this one small human. "Yes, I did steal away the soul of Sergudai Fiyanggo—but what concern is that of yours? I have stolen nothing that belongs to you."

"You have stolen nothing that belongs to me, but you had no right to steal away the life of a boy whose time had not yet come."

At that, Monggoldai Nakcu, powerful demon-spirit though he was, hung his head. "I was merely obeying a command from my lord, Ilmun Han, Lord of the Underworld. This is a sweet, handsome boy, this Sergudai Fiyanggo, and Ilmun Han wishes to keep him as his son."

"Then it is Ilmun Han I need to see," the Nisan Shaman said, and set out for the ruler's city. But the gates were locked fast and the walls were firm and tall. There was no way for even the mightest of shamans to enter. So Teteke began to chant, calling to all the spirits of the birds:

Kerani kerani Great soaring bird
Kerani kerani flying hawk
Kerani kerani mighty eagle,
Kerani kerani fly into the city and bring him out!
Kerani kerani Lift him out, fly him out!

The bird-spirits flew over the walls of the city. They soared down to where Sergudai Fiyanggo played in a garden, caught him up and flew away with him. Teteke took the boy by the hand, and the two began to run from there.

But Ilmun Han learned of the theft and summoned Monggoldai Nakcu to him, roaring, "How dare you fail me?"

"Master, please don't blame me. This is surely the doing of the Nisan Shaman. I will go after her."

He sped off and soon had all but overtaken Teteke and the boy. "Wait a bit, shaman!" he called. "Listen to me! Ilmun Han is furious, and he blames me! You can't take the boy without even paying a fee!"

"If you wish a fee," Teteke said coldly, "well and good. But if this is a challenge, so be it."

"No, no, no challenge! But if you could pay me just a little bit ... maybe some of that bean paste? And some of that paper?"

Teteke gave him three lumps of bean paste and three bundles of paper. "Now leave us alone."

"Ah well, this is fine for me. But it isn't quite enough, not for my master."

"What, then? I will not give you the boy!"

"The dog, then. Yes, and the rooster. Ilmun Han has no dogs to help him hunt, nor a rooster to crow for him. He would be pleased with these things, very pleased."

"Agreed. But first you must give the boy an increase in his life's span."

"Shaman, shaman, for you and you alone: I'll add twenty years to his life."

"Since he was stolen as a mere drooling child, twenty years is nothing."

"All right, then, thirty years."

"Since he was stolen before his mind had grown, thirty years is not enough."

"Then ... forty years."

"Since he was stolen before he could received any honors, forty years is not enough."

They bargained back and forth till at last Monggoldai Nakcu cried, "Very well, very well, I will add ninety years to his life span! He will have a nice, long life and raise fine children and stay in good health. But I cannot give you any more!"

"Agreed," the Nisan Shaman said sweetly. Giving him the dog and rooster, she went on her way with the boy's hand in hers.

But here was the one she had not wished to meet: her late husband. He stood boiling a cauldron of oil and glared at her. "Fickle Teteke, fickle wife, you revive all the others yet leave me here. Bring me back to life, or this cauldron shall be your fate!"

Teteke pleaded with him, "I did not leave you here by choice! I had no full powers then, no way to bring you back to life. You have been dead so long you have no body to which you may return. Listen to me, let me pass and I will burn much paper money over your grave."

But her husband's spirit cried, "You hated me when I was alive! You hate me now! Why should I let you pass?"

Teteke straightened in anger. "When you lived, how did you treat me? Like a slave! What did you leave me? Nothing! What did you leave your mother? Poverty! I have all this time protected her, cared for her, which you never did in all your life! Hear me, husband:

> *Denikun denikun Let us test your strength,*
> *Denikun denikun see if your corpse's strength has waned.*
> *Denikun denikun I call the spirits.*
> *Denikun denikun Take my husband in your claws.*
> *Denikun denikun Take him to Fungtu*
> *Denikun denikun deepest city of the Underworld.*
> *Denikun denikun Let him not return to human life!*

Her power was stronger than her husband's hate. The bird- spirits carried him away and Teteke saw him no more. She chanted in joy:

> *Deyangku deyangku Without a husband I'll be happy.*
> *Deyangku deyangku Free and happy to live as I will.*
> *Deyangku deyangku Facing the years*
> *Deyangku deyangku I shall be happy!*

Chanting, she brought Sergudai back the way she had come, back at last to the house of Baldu Bayan. Her assistant helped her back into her body, rousing her with incense, and she fanned Sergudai's soul back into its body. He sat up slowly, saying, "I have been asleep for so long. And what strange dreams I've had!"

Baldu Bayan and his wife laughed with joy. "Thank you, lady," they cried, "thank you. You have given us back our lives!"

"And my own," Teteke said softly, "and my own."

Chitoku

A Magician from Japan

Chitoku was both a monk and a diviner, a magician able to see into the future, and work wonders. Maybe he was no longer young, but that little fact was hardly enough to stop Chitoku from using his power to defend those who couldn't help themselves.

One day Chitoku was strolling along the beach, leaning lightly on his staff, when he came upon three men lying exhausted on the sand. They were still dripping with water; clearly they had just managed to pull themselves from the waves.

"What has happened?" Chitoku asked. "There's been no storm, no sign of any shipwreck. What happened to you?"

"Pirates," groaned one man. "I am—I was a merchant, the owner of a fine ship." He pulled himself wearily to his feet. "We were sailing home, loaded with a splendid cargo. But then the pirates attacked us. We fought back, my poor men and I, but there were too many of the scum. They slew all my men, save for these two servants. We just barely escaped with our lives by jumping overboard while the pirates were busy killing the wounded."

He buried his head in his hands, weeping. "My poor men are all lost. And I—I am ruined. That ship was the only one I owned. Its cargo was going to restore my fortunes. Now, ah now I have nothing!"

"I cannot restore your poor men to life," Chitoku said. "That is far beyond any man's powers. But as for everything else, well now, I can certainly help you with that."

The merchant looked at him, at this old man leaning on his staff, and bowed politely to hide his disbelief. "I will be glad of any aid."

"And you don't believe I can do as I say. Well now, you shall learn, indeed you shall. Come, we will return to the city."

The merchant's eyes widened a bit the next day when he saw a fisherman lend Chitoku a boat without so much as a question. They widened quite a bit more when he saw some of the city guards follow Chitoku back down to the beach without so much as a question.

"Come, into the boat," Chitoku told the merchant. "We must row out to the exact spot where the attack took place."

So they did, or at least to as close to the spot as the owner could remember. "Is this the time of day when the attack took place?" Chitoku asked.

"Yes, but—"

"Yes? Splendid." Leaning over the boat, the monk traced mysterious signs over the water and murmured mysterious words. The merchant waited, wondering. Surely something dramatic was going to happen!

But all that happened was that Chitoku sat back in the boat with a satisfied grunt. "Now, row us back to shore. We have some waiting to do."

It took some waiting, indeed. It took a full seven days. But at last a sail appeared on the horizon. As the ship drew nearer to shore, the merchant cried, "That's them! That's the pirates!"

The guards rowed out and pulled in the pirate ship.

"But—but what's wrong with the pirates?" the merchant cried. "They're not even trying to fight! They can't all be drunk, can they? So drunk they can't even draw a sword?"

"Not exactly," Chitoku said.

The pirate ship was heavy in the water with all the cargo they'd stolen. The merchant was so relieved he nearly wept.

"But what about the pirates?" the guards wanted to know. "We should kill them!"

"No," Chitoku told them. "There is no honor in slaying spellbound men. Turn them over to me."

He eyed the pirates as sternly as a father staring at erring children, and not a one of them could meet his gaze. "Do not do anything like that again," Chitoku scolded, and the pirates winced like guilty children. "Do you understand me? Yes? Good. Remember that it is only through me that you were taken—and that it is only through me that you still have your lives. Remember that there is one old monk on this shore who you'd better not meet again! Now, get away from here."

The pirates sailed hastily away and, sure enough, were never seen in that land again.

The Blind Fortune-teller

A Magician from Korea

Once, in the city of Hanyang, now known as Seoul, there lived a very skillful fortune-teller. No one knew his name or anything else about him, save for this fact: the fortune-teller was quite blind. But blindness was hardly a problem for him or a bar for his powers. Though ordinary sight was denied to him, the fortune-teller could see the magical world quite clearly, and the real world by way of magic.

One day, when the fortune-teller was in the marketplace, he saw, to his horror, a troop of demons laughing cruelly and making ugly gestures at everyone, sure that no human could see them. Suddenly they turned and began following a group of servants carrying food from the marketplace.

"They've chosen a victim," the fortune-teller murmured to himself. "And that victim lives in whatever household sent out those servants."

The fortune-teller followed the procession of humans and demons to a nobleman's elegant house, his magical sight leading him clearly. Though he saw the demons vanish at the house's main gate, the fortune-teller knew they hadn't left. Almost at once, he heard a terrified scream ring out, followed by a storm of frightened shouting.

"The demons have their victim!" The fortune-teller beat at the gate, calling to the guards he knew were standing within.

The gate opened a crack. "Go away, stranger," a guard snapped. "Go away. Our master's daughter has suddenly died."

"Ah, I knew it!" The fortune-teller pushed at the gate, trying to open it wider. "Let me in, I beg you. Take me to her. Yes, yes, I know I look like no one much, a plain blind man, but I am a true fortune-teller; I know what's happened, and I can help the poor girl—but only if you let me in!"

"I don't know ..."

"What have you to lose? Please, the longer we wait, the firmer hold the demons will have on the girl's soul! Let me in!"

So frantic was he and so determined did he sound that the guard let him in. The fortune-teller rushed without any hesitation straight for the dead girl's bedside, but the nobleman blocked his path. "Do you claim to revive the dead?"

"She is not truly dead. And yes, I can revive her—but only if we hurry!"

The nobleman hesitated only a moment. This blind stranger might be a charlatan, but then again, his powers might be real. There is no time for doubts.

There lay the poor girl's body. "Take it to a small room," the fortune-teller commanded, "an easily-sealed room."

It was done, and the body was placed on a mat. The fortune-teller went over every bit of the room himself, making sure that doors and windows were shut, pasting paper sheets over every possible crack. When he was done, he was sealed into the room with the body—not even smoke could escape.

"Not even demons," the fortune-teller corrected grimly, and began to chant.

Almost at once, the girl's body began to stir. The demons felt the power in that chant, and they didn't like it! But the fortune-teller only chanted more loudly. Now the demons were groaning with pain, feeling magic pulling at them, tearing them from the body. They shrieked and roared, trying to make the fortune-teller's smooth chant stumble, because once it was broken, his magic would fail.

But the fortune-teller never stumbled. The chant continued smoothly, growing ever louder, ever stronger. And with cries of fury, the demons fled the body. But there was no way out of the room, none at all! The magic chant began to tear them apart, destroying them—

Alas, just then one small servant girl outside the room grew so curious to know what was happening that she tore open a hole, just the tiniest of holes, in a piece of the paper covering a crack, hoping to see into the room.

What she saw was nothing, for the demons raced through that tiny hole like a sudden mighty gust of wind, bowling her over.

In the room, though, the once-dead girl blinked and stirred and opened her eyes. "I—I had the strangest dream," she murmured.

The fortune-teller called for the room to be unsealed. The girl's parents rushed in, full of joy.

"We will give you anything you ask!" they cried to the fortune-teller. "We will make you wealthy!"

"No. I want nothing. I have not long to live."

"But—but how can this be?"

"I could have destroyed the demons, had a hole not been torn in the paper. I could have destroyed them, but now I fear they will destroy me."

News of the fortune-teller's deed swept through the city, all the way to the royal palace. The king, however, was a shrewd, cynical man, the sort who believes in nothing that cannot be touched or measured. He had started a campaign to rid his city of all trickery. "And here is yet another case," he said, and ordered his guards to bring the fortune-teller to him.

"You claim to possess magic powers," the king said.

"I was born with certain gifts," the fortune-teller told him. "Some call them magic."

"You are blind, yet you see."

"I see without eyes, that is true."

"Bah! Come with me." The king had already commanded his servants to place a dead rat in the center of the room. "There," the king snapped. "What is lying on the floor before you?"

"Why, nothing but a dead rat!" the fortune-teller said in surprise. But then he frowned. "No. Not one. Three. Three rats are before us."

"You charlatan!" the king roared. "There is but one rat! Guards, take this fool away and have him beheaded."

But as the guards dragged the fortune-teller away, a curious courtier examined the rat. "Your Majesty," he said warily, "I think the fortune-teller was right."

"What? How so?"

"There are two baby rats inside this one."

"Three!" the king gasped. "Three rats—the fortune-teller was telling the truth. Guards, hurry! The execution must be stopped!"

But as the guards raced to the place of execution, a gust of wind blew them back. When they tried to shout to the executioner, the wind tore the words from their mouths.

The axe fell. There was a great roar of demonic laughter.

But then the laughter suddenly stopped. Was it that now the demons were happy with their revenge? Or was it that now the evil beings realized too late that the fortune-teller and his powers were no longer bound by a mortal body?

Shee Yee

A Magician from the Hmong of Laos

Shee Yee was born Tong Ntyai, and grew to be a young man, never guessing the magical destiny that would be his. Instead of magic, he sought music, and traveled from the land of men to the land of dragons in order to learn the stringed instrument known as the *qeng*. But while he was there, an evil spirit-woman left a giant egg in the human realm—an egg that hatched out all manner of evil spirits who roamed the land, devouring people.

So Tong Ntyai abandoned his peaceful dreams. Instead of staying in the land of dragons, he went on to the land of magic. There, he studied with the great sorcerer Pa La See. Three years he spent with the sage, and at the end of those years, had proven himself an apt pupil and swift learner. He could change his form at will, from man to beast or to mist, and could even heal those at the edge of death. Tong Ntyai had become a true magician, and took a new name, a magician's name. He became Shee Yee.

Now Shee Yee set out for the land of men, bearing a shaman's sword at his waist and carrying a gold-and-silver crossbow with arrows of iron and copper. As soon as he reached the land of men, he saw the evil spirits and began his attack, firing arrow after arrow. Each one struck its mark, and every spirit struck died on the spot. Shee Yee slew all but two of the evil spirits, for those two, hiding in a cave in a rocky mountain, seemed invulnerable to his arrows.

The evil spirits sent Shee Yee a letter, a most politely worded letter: "You are most powerful, most terrible. We would like to speak with you, to dine with you."

Shee Yee saw the message behind the message. These evil spirits wished to lull him off his guard, then kill him. So he refused. But the evil spirits continued to send their seemingly peaceful letters.

He wasn't worried only for himself. Before Shee Yee had gone off to the land of magic, he had wed a young woman. Though she was as clever as he, she had no magic. Shee Yee worried that the evil spirits might attack his wife when he was away. So the magician set out a basket of iron balls and filled a great piece of bamboo, ten times as long as a man is tall, with tobacco. He told his wife, "If I am away and the evil spirits come to plague you, tell them this: 'Before I may leave with you, you must eat what Shee Yee eats.' Give them the basket of iron balls to eat. If they succeed in eating them, say, 'Before I may leave with you, you must smoke Shee Yee's pipe.' And if they succeed in that, too, then say to them, 'Before I may leave with you, you must draw and load Shee Yee's crossbow.'"

"And that," his wife said cheerfully, "I doubt they can do!"

But sure enough, Shee Yee was called away to heal some sick folk. Soon after he'd left, down came the two evil spirits to ask his wife, "Where is Shee Yee?"

"He is treating the sick."

"He is afraid of us!" the evil spirits laughed. "Now you must come with us."

Shee Yee's wife smiled demurely. "I would be willing. But my husband told me that first you must prove that you're as strong as he. You must eat what he eats or I cannot go with you."

She showed them the basket of iron balls. To her horror, the evil spirits crunched down the iron balls, every one of them. "How powerful Shee Yee must be!" they said. "He eats the same things we do." Then they turned to Shee Yee's wife. "Now you must come with us."

"No, no, wait," she said hastily. "First you must prove you can smoke the same pipe he smokes."

The evil spirits laughed. "So be it," said the larger of the two. "Give me the pipe."

Shee Yee's wife dragged out the long length of tobacco-filled bamboo. To her horror, the evil spirit took one deep breath, and all the tobacco was gone in one great cloud of smoke. "There," the evil spirit said. "I have smoked Shee Yee's pipe. Now you must come with us."

"Wait, wait. Before I may come with you, Shee Yee said that first you must prove you can draw and load his cross-bow. This is what my husband said, you understand."

"Give me the crossbow," the larger evil spirit said. "I will draw it." To the horror of Shee Yee's wife, the evil spirit snatched up the gold and silver crossbow as though it was a child's toy and drew it far past the trigger, indeed all the way to the end of the stock itself! Dropping the crossbow, the evil spirit snarled, "Now you will come with us!"

With that, the evil spirits carried her away.

That night, Shee Yee returned to find the doors to his home standing ajar. The bowl that had held the iron balls was empty, the tube of bamboo was empty. Ha, and here lay his crossbow, drawn all the way to the end of the stock!

"The evil spirits were too strong," he muttered. "But I will not let them take my wife!"

He unstrung the crossbow, snatched up a handful of arrows, and hurried off toward the mountain cave of the evil spirits. It was fully dark by the time Shee Yee had climbed up there, and he was able to hide in the shadows. There sat the two evil spirits before a fire, their backs to him, and there was his wife sitting to one side. Shee Yee hastily drew his crossbow and fired, straight at the larger of the evil spirits.

But the arrow bounced harmlessly off. "Ouch!" the spirit said. "A spark from the fire stung me."

Biting his lip, Shee Yee aimed this time at the smaller evil spirit. But this arrow bounced harmlessly off the other spirit as well. "Ouch!" the spirit cried. "A spark got me, too!"

"Bad fire!" the larger spirit snapped. "Pop and spark all you want, but don't you dare bother us again or we shall kill you!"

Shee Yee, seeing that his arrows were useless, slipped back into hiding. If the spirits were invulnerable to iron arrowheads, he must hunt for a spell that would kill the spirits yet not harm his wife!

Meanwhile, Shee Yee's wife was busy. "My, how big and strong you two are!" she cooed. "I'm amazed something as small as a spark of fire could hurt you."

The evil spirits snorted. "That? That hardly touched us. Listen, woman, we are truly invulnerable, the two of us. Even Shee Yee with that pretty crossbow of his couldn't kill us."

Shee Yee's wife pretended wide-eyed admiration. "But—but surely *something* can harm you."

The larger evil spirit shrugged. "My own iron crossbow might. Have you seen it? It is eight arm-spans long and nine arm-spans wide. But even if it were fired directly at me, I still would not be harmed unless magic words were recited first. And even then I would not be harmed unless whoever said the magic words and fired the arrow caught me before I have bathed in the lake out there. Once I have bathed in that lake, nothing in the world can harm me."

"Aren't you *clever?*" Shee Yee's wife cooed. "But you must teach me the magical words. Otherwise, if my husband comes here and you haven't had time yet to bathe, I won't be able to help you."

So sweetly did she coo that the evil spirit muttered, "Very well," and taught her the magic words.

That morning, the evil spirits went off to work harm. Shee Yee stole into the cave. "Are you all right, my dear?"

"Yes, yes, and I've learned how we may be rid of the evil spirits!"

Quickly, Shee Yee's wife told him of the lake and the crossbow and the magic words. Together, husband and wife dragged the heavy iron crossbow down to the lake. The evil spirits had come here to bathe for so many years that the shore had turned red as blood and smooth as stone. Shee Yee and his wife hid themselves and the crossbow behind a tree and waited. Sure enough, here came the smaller of the two evil spirits. Shee Yee and his wife struggled to draw the heavy crossbow. Shee Yee said the magic words and let the arrow fly—and the smaller evil spirit fell dead into the lake, which began to boil.

The boiling quieted. Shee Yee and his wife drew the iron crossbow a second time and waited. Here came the larger of the two evil spirits. Again Shee Yee said the magic words and let the arrow fly—and the larger evil spirit fell dead into the lake. Shee Yee and his wife left the boiling lake, lugging the iron crossbow between them.

Alas, in the struggle with the heavy crossbow, they accidentally fired an arrow. It shot through a mountain and cut right through the ladder leading to the realm of Nzeu Nyong, ruler of all evil spirits. He looked out from his realm and saw Shee Yee and knew instantly what the magician had done.

"Kill evil spirits, will he?"

Nzeu Nyong brooded and plotted. And at last Nzeu Nyong sent a whole family of evil spirits, nine brothers in all, to the land of men. They hid in the mountains one day, waiting for Shee Yee.

The magician was on his way home after healing the sick when the nine evil spirits sprang out of hiding and surrounded him.

"Where do you think you're going?"

"Home," Shee Yee said. "I've been healing the sick all day."

"You healed the sick but you killed two of our kind! Now we're going to see who is stronger, you or us!"

The oldest evil brother promptly turned into a water buffalo and charged. Shee Yee quickly turned into a water buffalo as well, and met the charge with lowered horns. The two buffaloes crashed together, head to head, kicking up great clouds of dust as they struggled, but neither could push the other away.

"Our brother is in trouble," the other evils spirits decided. "We must help him."

They turned into eight water buffalos and charged Shee Yee. Just in time, he saw his danger and turned back to human-form, drawing his shaman's sword. It flashed and slashed, sharp as lightning, and with every slash, another evil spirit was cut apart.

Alas, the spirits could not be slain that way. Each time Shee Yee cut a spirit apart, it reformed and attacked anew. Wearying, Shee Yee turned into a cloud and floated up into the sky. The evil spirits then merged into a fierce wind and roared after him, trying to tear the cloud apart. Shee Yee quickly turned into a drop of water and let himself fall.

But one of the evil spirits saw this and turned into a leaf to catch the drop. Shee Yee landed on the leaf, but quickly turned into a dee racing off before he could be caught. The nine spirits turned to a wolf pack, snarling and baying after him.

"I can't run much further," Shee Yee thought. "I—I must rest."

He saw a rat's burrow and quick as thought became a rat, diving into shelter. The nine spirits were tired, too, but the oldest of them saw Shee Yee dive into the burrow.

"If he's become a rat, then I shall be a cat!"

Shee Yee rested until he'd caught his breath. Then, seeing the cat looming over the burrow, he transformed himself into a spiny caterpillar and started to creep out.

"I see you!" the cat-spirit cried, and pounced. But the spines of the caterpillar hurt his mouth. He spat Shee Yee out, right back into the burrow.

"Smaller," Shee Yee decided, and turned himself into a tiny red ant. He scurried out of the burrow, nipping the cat on the tail in passing. The cat whirled, saw no one, and went back to watching the burrow, sure that Shee Yee was still within.

Meanwhile, Shee Yee made it to his home, where he told his wife, "I'm late because nine evil spirit brothers ambushed me. No, I'm not hurt. But I must stop them before they come after me again. Quickly, make me a nice meal, something that can be carried easily."

So his wife made a nice meal of soy bean curd and rice and packed it up. Shee Yee knew that evil spirits are often attracted to pretty women, so he instantly became a pretty young maid and set out again. He found the home of the nine spirit brothers. There they sat, all nine together.

"This is my chance to get all nine at one blow," Shee Yee thought; he sauntered inside. "My, what fine-looking brothers!" he cooed, fluttering his eyelashes at them. "I shall prepare a fine meal for you."

"Yes, yes, and then we shall play," the evil spirits cried.

"Then we shall play, indeed."

None of the evil spirits noticed what Shee Yee was doing. They were too busy crowing and congratulating each other on how well the day had turned out after all. Shee Yee set up a central basin of oil, just as though he really was a girl meaning to cook a meal, and started a fire burning under it, but he was muttering spells under his breath.

"What are you saying?" the evil spirits asked.

"Oh, nothing, nothing," Shee Yee assured them.

He took a mouthful of water, then spat it at the hot oil. The oil blazed up into spears of flame stabbing the evil spirits. The spirits burst like empty sacks: Boom, boom, boom, boom, boom, boom, boom, boom.

"Eight?" Shee Yee thought as he fled the burning house. "What happened to the ninth brother?"

Though Shee Yee didn't know it, the ninth brother, the youngest brother, had managed to creep into a crack in the floor and hide there. He was untouched by the fire, and he meant to get revenge on Shee Yee! And so, when it was safe, he turned himself into a green hawk.

The magician hurried home. But as he was going through the mountains, the green hawk dove down at him. "Ah, so here's the ninth brother!" Shee Yee said, and sprang aside. "Wait, wait," he called to the hawk, "not so quickly! There must be a certain style to these combats. I see that you can transform yourself into pretty shapes. But I don't believe a green hawk has any strength. No, no, a hawk can never have any strength."

"I *am* strong!" the spirit insisted.

"I doubt it. After all, you're only the youngest brother of nine. No, you have no strength at all."

"I do! I do!"

"Shall we test it? Come, see if you can shatter this rock. If you can, then I will surrender to you."

That sounded fine to the green hawk. He soared up and up, then dove down and down. He hit the rock squarely, splitting it in half. But the hawk-spirit also knocked himself out. Shee Yee quickly pulled out some of the hawk's feathers, then whispered a charm over the rock, making it whole once more.

The hawk stirred. "Did I do it? Did I split the rock?"

"I'm afraid not. Look."

The hawk-spirit groaned. "Let me try again."

He soared up and up again, then dove down and down. Again he hit the rock squarely, again he split it, and again knocked himself out. Shee Yee took another handful of feathers, then whispered his charm over the rock, making it whole once more.

The evil spirit never suspected a trick. He dove at the rock again and again, and each time Shee Yee took another handful of feathers. At last the groggy hawk-spirit tried to take off for one last try at that stubborn rock—but Shee Yee had taken so many feathers that the hawk couldn't get off the ground.

The magician drew his shaman's sword and started forward. "Wait, wait, wait," the hawk-spirit begged. "Don't kill me. Please, please, don't kill me."

Shee Yee paused. He'd never intended to kill the hawk-spirit. "Very well," he said severely. "But you must swear this vow: You must swear to chase away other hawks, yes, and eagles as well, from people's crops and herds. In exchange, you may have all the rats and mice you can catch."

"And a nice, fat chick now and then?"

Shee Yee sighed. "And a nice, fat chick now and then. But *only* now and then. If I hear that you have been breaking your vow ..." He touched the hilt of his shaman's sword and frowned.

"No, no, no," the hawk-spirit cried. "I will be a good green hawk. I will drive off the other hawks and eagles. I will protect the people's crops and herds."

And so the green hawk does even to this day.

Shee Yee went home. There would be other battles with evil; he was sure of it. But for now, for now, there was peace.

Djunban

A Magician from Australia

*D*junban was a tall man, powerfully built, his beard full and black. He was a rainmaker and thunder-bringer, leader of his people, but none can say from where his powers came. Those powers even included this strangeness: he carried people—spirit people perhaps, though no one knows for certain what they were—he carried those strange people under his skin.

Djunban was going along one day, seeking his human people, his clan, who had gone on ahead of him. They wandered freely since they were used to his going apart from them from time to time, and had no doubt that he would be able to rejoin them.

Djunban owned one very valuable thing, a boomerang with such magic that it never failed to bring down game, to kill that game, whenever he threw it. When he regained his people by a waterhole after their long, wearying travel, he found them hungry and went in search of game, taking the boomerang.

But alas, Djunban's sister, Mandjia, not realizing that her brother was nearby, had gone to gather roots. When Djunban threw his boomerang, it hit the nearest target—it hit Mandjia on the leg. She fell and lay still, sorely wounded, and Djunban ran to her side. He sang lightness into her limp body so that he could carry her back to the people for tending, then returned to hunt for his boomerang. For all his shock over what had just happened, he dared not lose so valuable a weapon.

But where was it? The sand was undisturbed; there were no holes into which it could have fallen. Djunban found tracks of other people. Had some other clan picked up the boomerang? There were some traces that another clan had passed nearby. No, he could not lose that boomerang! Even though worry for Mandjia and for his clan was strong in his mind, Djunban set out on the trail of the other clan.

At last he found them, and they were one that was friendly with his own. They had no argument with him, not even when Djunban insisted they all show him their boomerangs.

Not one of the weapons was his. Dejected, Djunban started back toward his own people. The air was still, the land was dry, and dust clouded him. He had spent too long hunting for his boomerang; the rain had not fallen for far too long. Djunban hurried now. He must bring rain, or the waterhole would dry up and his people suffer!

Ah, this was the right thing to think, this worry, for as Djunban went, his foot kicked against something. The boomerang! Had its tricky magic hidden it all this while? Had it, maybe, even been ashamed for having taken a human for game? Djunban, unable to find the answer, picked it up and hurried on.

Yes, there were his people, his clan. And yes, the waterhole was all but dry. Djunban knew he'd returned just in time.

But sadly, his sister Mandjia, had died. The boomerang slew whatever it brought down, and so it was for her as well.

There was no chance to mourn, not yet. First there must be rain. Djunban removed the spirit people from under his skin and began to dance, signalling to the people, spirit and real, to dance with him. At last they collapsed, too weary to continue, but Djunban continued, chanting his rain magic:

Nganggali bada-djara
Rurgu djuna nganggali,
Stormy clouds,
Thundering ...

He continued his song, and the air grew thick and heavy. Great clouds billowed up from nowhere. Djunban scraped a *garalba* shell, one of his magical aids, scraped a piece free, put it in his mouth, spit it out.

And the rains came. The people were saved.

But that clan, like other clans, could not stay in one site for long. The land was too barren, even with that waterhole; it could not support them. They travelled on. But they left the body of Mandjia, Djunban's sister behind.

She stayed in his thoughts, though, she stayed in his heart. Guilt over her death haunted him, and so this tale comes to a tragic end. For Djunban, bringing rain for his people again, was too lost in memory to notice what he did. He cut off too large a piece of the *garalba* shell. Before Djunban knew it, he had ground away fully half of the shell and worked his magic with far too much force. The rain came in torrents, too quickly, too fiercely for the dry desert soil to drink it in. The flood waters rose with deadly speed, and they drowned Djunban beneath a sea of mud.

Kukali

A Magician from Hawaii

Kukali was the son of a great *kahuna,* a priest of the Polynesian people and a man of vast wisdom. When he saw that Kukali had the gift for magic, he taught the boy well. Kukali learned the proper prayers to please the gods and the proper charms to defeat his enemies. He learned the ways of canoes and weapons, too, and which omens were good or ill.

As Kukali grew to manhood and gained full control of his powers, his father smiled and handed him a banana. "Eat what you will of this. But whatever you do, save the skin."

Of course Kukali promptly ate the banana and saved the skin, just to see what would happen. And what happened was this: a new banana was instantly within the skin.

"This is wonderful!" Kukali cried. Like many of his people, he had the longing to explore the seas, yet was limited by the few supplies that could be packed into a canoe. "Now I can explore all the islands, all the seas, go as far as I wish yet have no fear of starvation."

So off Kukali went to the forest and built himself a fine, swift canoe by magic chants. Off he set in his canoe, the magic banana with him, and explored the seas as he would. Many days passed, and at last Kukali grew weary. He beached his canoe on a peaceful shore and settled down to sleep.

But as Kukali slept, a monster flew overhead, a terrible bird-demon, Halulu. Each feather of his mighty wings ended in a talon, and he was forever hungry. He saw the sleeping Kukali. Swooping down, he carried the young man away so carefully that Kukali never woke.

When Kukali did wake, he found himself, to his astonishment, no longer lying on the beach beside his canoe. He was in a tiny valley with no apparent exit but the sky and cliffs that towered up like the walls of a prison. Nor was he trapped in this valley alone. Here were all those people Halulu had captured and was storing as the bird-demon's larder. For Halulu liked his meat dead, and perched above the valley every day, waiting for another man or woman to collapse of starvation. As soon as someone collapsed, the bird-demon would sweep a wing down over the valley. Those still strong enough to escape the sweep of those terrible taloned feathers survived. Those too weak to move were snagged and carried off for Halulu's meal.

Kukali looked about at the starving captives. "Don't fear," he told them. "We still live."

He shared the fruit of the magic banana with them and smiled to see them grow strong. He taught them how to make sharp-edged spears and knives from the rocks about them. While they practiced with their new weapons, Kukali practiced his strongest spells.

Meanwhile, Halulu was growing hungry. But every time the monstrous bird-demon swept a wing over the valley, his taloned feathers came away empty. There were no dying humans to be snared! Raging, famished, Halulu tried again and yet again but caught no dinner.

"Be alert," Kukali whispered to the captives. "Halulu will try one last sweep of his wing. We must be ready!"

Here came the sweep of the terrible wing. Kukali and the others sprang out of hiding, slashing at the taloned feathers with their sharp stone tools. The wing was destroyed, the feathers cut to bits. Halulu screamed with pain and rage and swept his other wing down into the valley—but it, too, was cut to bits. Halulu, shrieking, hurled himself down into the valley, sharp-taloned, powerful feet outstretched. Kukali quickly chanted powerful spells that threw Halulu sideways, and the captives cut the bird-demon himself to bits.

"The terrible Halulu is dead!" they cried.

"Not yet," Kukali said. "We must burn his body in a fire. And the only way to do that is to cast down trees from the top of the cliffs."

"But how can we get up there?" the people asked. "How are we to get out of this valley?"

Kukali carved magic footholds in the sheer cliffs. The captives made ropes out of vines and climbed to freedom. They cut down trees with their stone tools, tossed them over Halulu, then threw down torches to burn the bird-demon to ash.

"*Now* Halulu is dead," Kukali said.

But two burning feathers caught the wind. They floated off to Halulu's sister, Namakeaha, kinswoman to Pele, goddess of the volcano fires. Namakeaha, who lived in a bottomless pit, saw these feathers drift down to her, smelled the smoke of their burning, and knew at once that Halulu was dead.

"He could only have been slain by a mighty magician. Who is this powerful *kapua*? Watch warily, my people."

Meanwhile, Kukali had bid farewell to those he'd rescued and set out to explore. He came to Namakeaha's realm and wondered what might lie in so deep and mysterious a pit. Fearlessly, he lowered himself by a vine rope. But Namakeaha's *kahunas*, her priests, cast a spell that cut the vine in half. Kukali fell, but as he fell, he called out a prayer, an incantation—

And thus he landed not on hard, unyielding rock but gently in a pool of healing water. Unharmed, he climbed out of the pool, only to be met by one of Namakeaha's *kahunas*. "Don't be alarmed," the priest told him. "I hold no emnity toward you. And I give you this warning: Eat nothing in this realm. All food here is poisonous to outsiders."

Kukali thanked him. With his magic banana, he had no need to eat other food. He had no wish to have enemies among these folk, so he went on into Namakeaha's realm. Some *kahunas* fought him, others befriended him, but at last he came to where Namakeaha sat. She was no monster like Halulu! She was a fine, handsome woman who told Kukali, "Come, brave one, sit and feast."

Kukali smiled. "I have my own feast. You need not waste your food."

Namakeaha was intrigued. No mortal man had ever come this way; no mortal man could have survived. Yet here was this brave magician, eating bananas as though he hadn't a care for his safety. She forgot to be angry over Halulu's death. After all, hadn't that bird-demon been an unpleasant member of the family? Weren't they all better without him?

So peace was sworn between Kukali and Namakeaha, peace and more. With time, they wed, and Kukali said to his new wife, "You deserve a finer realm than this dark pit. Come with me to the islands and the sunlight."

So she sailed with him away from the darkness, and they lived happily together in the light.

Tsak

A Magician from the Tsimshian of British Columbia

Tsak was a tricky, clever youngster—necessarily clever since he was an orphan with only a grandmother for family. Tsak survived by tricking and plotting his way along until even his grandmother grew angry at his deceptions and drove him away to find his own life.

Sad and lonely, Tsak wandered through the heavy cedar forest, not knowing where to go. But there before him a man suddenly appeared, a giant who asked, "What is this sorrow?"

Warily, Tsak invented a tale, saying, "The Wolf clan people attacked my own and stole all our food."

Did the giant believe him? Perhaps. Perhaps not. But the giant never questioned what he was told. Instead, he said, "You are meant to be a shaman, and that you shall be. Take this pebble, but use it carefully. If you put it in your mouth and wish, whatever you wish will occur. Take this bow and this quiver of arrows, as well. It will make you a fine hunter."

Tsak took the bow and quiver of arrows, and the giant disappeared into the forest without a sound. Tsak hunted, and found that the arrows never missed. He brought as much meat as he could carry back to his people, and made peace with them all.

But now Tsak was restless. He had these new shamanistic powers, didn't he? He had bird and animal helpers who would do his bidding. And yet where was the quest worthy of a shaman?

Then Tsak heard a tale of a princess, said to be the most beautiful woman in the world, who lived in a village so high in the mountains that it nearly touched the sky. Many men had tried to win her, but all had died, slain by her father, the great Chief-of-the-Sky.

"I will see this princess," Tsak decided. "And if I like her, I will win her."

He called one of his bird helpers, a robin, and asked, "How may I travel to where the beautiful princess lives?"

"You must first learn to fly," the robin told him. "And that you can do by making a magic robe from the skin of a loon."

Tsak took his bow and quiver of arrows and hunted until he found a large enough loon, which he quickly killed and skinned. He dried the skin and tanned it carefully, making sure that none of the feathers were damaged, and added magic to it. When Tsak was done, he had a garment that would let him fly.

"This is wonderful," Tsak said, swooping over the trees, "but now I need to know where to fly."

"It is a long journey," the robin told him, "even by wing. But I will guide you there."

They flew and they flew, and at last came to a mighty mountain, one that reached up till it nearly touched the sky. "The village of the beautiful princess is up there," the robin said. "I cannot fly so high."

"I can," Tsak told him, and started up.

But it was a very mighty mountain. Midway there, Tsak began to wonder if he was going to make it. He struggled on, up and up. But the winds were strong near the mountain's top. They hurled him against the side of the mountain till at last he fell, and only his magic kept Tsak from being dashed to pieces. Even so, he lay stunned and bleeding for some time.

Tsak was still only half-awake when he felt someone pinch his thigh and whisper, "Wake up. Wake up!"

Tsak opened one eye. "No one there," he muttered. "Must have dreamed it."

He went back to sleep, but someone pinched his thigh again, harder this time, and whispered, "Wake up! My grandmother wants to see you."

Tsak opened both eyes. He still didn't see anyone!

Yes, he did. A little grey mouse sat wiggling its whiskers at him. "My grandmother wants to see you," it repeated.

Tsak followed the mouse to a tiny house, into which he just managed to squeeze. A little mouse woman sat there. "Good," she said. "I have been waiting for you. You wish to reach the beautiful princess. But there is only one way to do this. Follow the trail just outside as far as it goes. You will reach a wall wherein is set a magic doorway that opens and shuts to crush any who try to enter. First, though, burn your earrings so that I may help you."

Tsak, being used to the strange ways of magic, took off his finely woven woolen earrings and tossed them into the mouse woman's fire. "That's good," she said. "Now, when you reach that dangerous door, you must wait and count each opening. When the doorway opens for the fourth time, fly inside as fast as you can move. Once you are safely past the doorway, you will find yourself in the village you seek. Remember to keep your magic pebble with you at all times, and you just might succeed."

Tsak thanked the mouse woman and went on his way. Sure enough, there was the wall, and there was the magic doorway. Tsak put on his loonskin robe, the waited, counting carefully. Ah, here was the fourth opening! He flew through—and found himself in a beautiful country. Ahead stood a huge house larger than any longhouse in his own country, and Tsak knew this must be the home of Chief-of-the-Sky.

And then he saw the most beautiful woman he had ever seen, followed by several attendants. Ah, this could only be the princess! And Tsak fell totally in love with her.

That night, Tsak stole into the house, his magic pebble making him invisible. There was the young woman, the lovely princess, asleep and whispering in her sleep, longing for a husband to love her.

"*I* love you," Tsak whispered, and she woke with a gasp. "Don't be afraid," he added, taking the pebble out of his mouth so that she could see him.

Well now, when Tsak wasn't worrying about playing a trick or working magic, he was a good-looking young man, his clever eyes set in a fine-featured face. The princess liked the look of him. And when they spoke together, whispering so that no one else would hear, she liked the quick, clever wit of him, too. They talked together for a time, then they embraced. And, in the custom of the people of those days, they wed there and then.

Now, in the morning, the chief was understandably amazed to find his daughter with her new husband. And, jealous of Tsak, and of Tsak's powers—since Chief-of-the-Sky was a shaman, too—the chief decided to be rid of his new son-in-law. So he pretended to greet Tsak warmly.

"We are in sore need of wood," he told the young man. "All the strong men must go out and cut down some trees for our village. You shall take with you these two great slaves to help you."

Tsak already suspected that this was a trick. After all, he'd played many a trick on folks himself! But he went off into the forest with the two great slaves and cut down a mighty tree. Then, since the tree must be broken up into manageable pieces, he took a wedge and hammer and split the tree in two. But as he was maneuvering between the two halves of the tree, the slaves quickly hammered out the wedge—the two halves snapped shut!

The slaves hurried back to the chief. "We have killed Tsak. He is surely crushed between the two halves of a tree."

But Tsak had placed the magic pebble in his mouth. He had become so small he'd slipped away from the trap. Now, his regular self again, he came strolling into the village, half the tree slung over his shoulder. "I will bring in the second half later. These two helpers of mine ran off and left me to do all the work."

The princess cried out with joy to see her husband alive and unharmed. Chief-of-the-Sky fumed, but could say nothing. Instead, he told Tsak, "Now we must hunt some seals, since our village needs meat. You must go, too."

There were the seals, swimming about by the sealing grounds. The men took out their great wooden canoes and caught a good many seals. One seal reared up out of the water, and Tsak speared it. But it began to pull his canoe right toward a huge whirlpool. This was the second of the traps set to slay Tsak. But he, suspecting just such a trap, placed his magic pebble in his mouth, became invisible so the seal could not see and avoid him, and slew it.

When the princess saw her husband returning from the hunt with good, fat seals, she laughed with joy. But Chief-of-the-Sky still fumed. One more trap, he thought, one more trap would slay this upstart young shaman.

"Tsak, we both have magic powers. So let there be a test between us to see which of us is the stronger shaman."

Tsak, who was growing tired of fending off traps, agreed. So Chief-of-the-Sky ordered his slaves to build a great fire and heat cooking stones within. When the stones were red hot, the slaves put them into a huge cooking pot filled with water. Soon that water was boiling hot.

"Here is the test, Tsak. Jump in there, into the boiling water. If your shaman powers are greater than mine, you will not be burned. If, however, mine are greater, farewell, Tsak!"

Tsak slipped the magic pebble into his mouth, and if he was worried, no one could tell. He jumped boldly into the boiling water.

"Hurry!" the chief snapped to his slaves. "Cover the pot!"

They did, and there it sat, bubbling fiercely over the fire. After a long while, Chief-of-the-Sky smiled thinly. "He must be well-done by now. Open the pot."

But there Tsak sat, calm as can be. "A chilly bath," he said, and jumped out.

"You've won," the chief admitted grudgingly. "Let there be peace between us."

But Tsak knew it wasn't wise to stay here and be a constant reminder of failure to his father-in-law. So he and the princess left that village and returned to Tsak's own. There, Tsak became chief, using his powers to rule wisely and cleverly. And, he and his wife lived happily together for all their days.

Taligvak

A Magician from the Copper Inuit of Canada

Taligvak was a young but very powerful shaman. Because of those powers, the rest of his tribe feared him, even though he had offered them no harm. As a result, Taligvak lived on the edge of society, poor in possessions and, since no woman dared approach, without a wife. He was not happy about being an outcast of his people, but at least there were the spirit-folk who came at his commands to keep him company.

Now, the people might have gone right on trying to ignore this poor but perilous shaman living on the edge of their society. But a terrible winter came, with storms so fierce no seal hunting could be done. And famine began to gnaw away at the village. There were other shamans, less powerful but also less perilous than Taligvak, so the people invited them to work their magics. But not one of the shamans could summon the seals.

"We must summon Taligvak," the people realized reluctantly.

Three men went to Taligvak's winter home, his igloo, but two were so afraid of what might lie within that they wouldn't even enter. The third man glanced nervously into the igloo and called, "Taligvak, the people need to speak with you. Will you come to them?"

Taligvak did not answer right away. He was thinking, of course, that the people only called to him when they wanted something from him. They never tried merely be-friending him. "The wind is fierce," he said at last, which was true. "I have nothing warm to wear." This was also true, since no one had ever traded their warm furs with him. "I will not come to them."

The three men hurried away, sure they were about to be turned into monsters. But nothing happened to them. When the people heard their words, they sent a brave young woman with a present of warm clothing, a parka, mittens, and boots. She took him gently by the arm and brought him to the people.

He stood silent as though turned to ice, there within the great igloo, the *qalgie* used by the people as a dancing place and assembly hall, his eyes chill as the wind. No one dared ask if he knew what they wanted from him: Of course a shaman such as he would know.

"You want a warm home," someone dared to say. "You want to stay with us."

And another added, "You want good clothes, warm furs. You want to be part of us. All these things will be yours if only you bring the seals back. We are starving!"

Taligvak turned and stalked outside. "Do not watch what I do," he called over his shoulder. "You stay in there and dance."

The people nervously began to sing and dance hunting songs to call the seals. Meanwhile, Taligvak studied the ice. It was thick, so thick none of the people had been able to cut through to the sea below. Taligvak knelt and blew on the ice, and the magic in his breath melted the ice right down to the sea.

"Continue to dance," he told the people. "Do not watch what I do."

He had a tiny harpoon in one hand, perfect as a toy. Holding it aloft, Taligvak called to the spirit world, to his spirit helpers, chanting of the joy of catching a fine, fat seal, of seeing it stretched out on the ice and knowing the famine was ended.

And the spirits brought a curious seal to the hole in the ice. The tiny harpoon was suddenly the size of a normal weapon. Taligvak harpooned the seal and pulled it to the surface. "Now, come!" he called to the people.

They hurried to take the seal and help him pull the harpoon from its body. Taligvak ordered that the seal be cut up and its meat distributed, then continued his hunting, repeating his magical chant until there were enough seals on the ice to feed all the people. The famine was ended, and everyone nearly wept for joy, knowing that now they would live through the winter. They praised Taligvak over and over.

However, they still feared Taligvak. In fact, they feared him even more now that they saw some of his power. By the time spring came and the people could leave their winter camp to hunt and fish inland, they would sometimes help Taligvak in daily chores. But he was still left mostly alone on the edge of society.

"If they have abandoned me," Taligvak decided, "I will abandon them."

The summer thaw set in. Taligvak went off totally by himself, alone on the tundra, the vast northern plains. He heard what the wind sang and heard the gladness in the cries of birds. Taligvak enjoyed that time of peace. He enjoyed watching the river flow and the caribou return, watching the plants grow, feeling the whole earth quicken with new life.

Food came easily. Taligvak built himself a kayak, not using his powers since magic was not meant for such ordinary things, but putting it together in the normal way from bits of wood, scraps of animal hide and lengths of animal sinew. He hunted caribou and caught fish and never lacked for food. Deciding on a place to live for the brief Arctic summer, he even built himself a comfortable house of stone on the firm tundra turf. Taligvak lived well, and barely missed the people who had abandoned him.

But Taligvak had not been forgotten. While he was living well, they were not. Was it magic? Was it Taligvak's power that he wasn't even deliberately using that was affecting their luck? For in all that rich summer, they caught no caribou, caught no fish. And even the plants they found were bitter and poorly nourishing. The famished people wandered far and further yet.

And at last they stumbled on Taligvak's home.

He recognized them at once, of course. And if he was shocked to see how starved they'd grown, Taligvak showed nothing of it on his face or in his eyes.

"Come," he said shortly. "I will feed you."

The plate he offered them was a scrap of hide they had thrown away. The food he offered them was a few sad scraps of meat and bone.

"Taligvak is suffering, too," the people whispered. "His powers must have failed him."

But then Taligvak began to sing magic over the plate. He sang about the caribou he'd hunted and the fish he'd caught. He sang food onto that plate till it overflowed. Not even all the people eating their fill could finish all that food.

"Have I lost my powers?" Taligvak asked.

"No," they all agreed, "no, you have not. Will you not come back to live with us?"

"No," Taligvak said.

He aided the people from time to time after that, but only when their need was greater than their ability to help themselves.

And Taligvak never did go back to them.

Spider Woman

A Magician from the Hopi of the American Southwest

Spider Woman was not born of mortal parents. Indeed, no one knows the details of her birth; she was simply there, a grown woman or (if the fancy took her) a spider, at the beginning of things, full of magic. She liked to wander among the people, helping this person, teaching that one. Spider Woman was, in fact, helping the Pinon Maidens, along with Mole, when Kwataka, Man-Eagle, first appeared.

Kwataka was a terrible monster, a merging, as his name implies, of bird and human, and he possessed all the worst aspects of both. He killed for the joy of it; Kwataka stole women away, then, when he grew bored with them, slew and ate them. And because whenever he left his mountain lair, he always wore a magical shirt, a flint-arrowhead shirt that no weapon could pierce, he had no fear of humans. Now Kwataka soared over the Hopi, just high enough over one particular village so that no one saw him, just low enough so he could watch one young woman who took his fancy. She was Lakone Mana, new wife of the young hero, Puukonhoya. Husband and wife were very much in love.

Kwataka knew nothing of love. What he wanted, he took. He swooped down, snatched up Lakone Mana, and soared back up into the sky before anyone on the ground realized what had happened. Puukonhoya cried out his wife's name in anguish. Sighting Kwataka's path in the sky, the warrior ran after him as best he could. But what earth-bound man could chase Kwataka?

But here sat Spider Woman with the Pinon Maidens. "Where are you going with such a rush, Puukonhoya?"

"Kwataka has stolen away my wife!"

"That is bad," Spider Woman agreed gently. "But it can be made better. I will help you. You, Pinon Maidens, gather pine resin. Make me an exact copy of Kwataka's flint-arrow-head shirt. Be quick about it!"

Sure enough, the Pinon Maidens quickly gathered the resin, and quickly made an exact copy of the flint-arrowhead shirt. "Excellent!" Spider Woman said. "Mole, make ready. We will need your help as well."

Mole agreed.

Spider Woman sprinkled sacred corn pollen over the shirt, chanting an invocation, then changed into her other true shape, becoming a tiny spider sitting on Puukonhoya's ear. "I'm here," she said in her now piping little voice. "Now, let us be off. Kwataka's lair is at the top of that mountain."

They reached the mountain, but Puukonhoya frowned with worry. "How can I get up there? I don't see any way to climb."

"No need," Spider Woman said in his ear. "Mole, dig us a tunnel, please."

Mole dug a tunnel into the mountain, sloping up and up. Puukonhoya, with Spider Woman on his ear, climbed up after Mole and found himself coming out of the mountain onto a ledge far above the ground. "But Kwataka's lair is higher still," Spider Woman said. "Now I shall call some good birds to help."

Several came. An eagle carried Spider Woman, Puukon-hoya and Mole part of the way up. When the eagle wearied, a grey hawk took them higher still. When the grey hawk wearied, a red hawk took them higher still, right to the white house on the mountain peak that was Kwataka's lair. Spider

Woman thanked the red hawk, as she had thanked the grey hawk and eagle.

"Wait," she said to Puukonhoya, who was about to climb the ladder into the white house. "You can't climb that yet! The rungs are lined with sharp obsidian, like row after row of terrible knives."

"Then what am I to do?"

"Wait for Horned Toad. Ah, here he is. Puukonhoya, pick some berries, please, and feed them to Horned Toad."

The young man did. Horned Toad chewed the berries into a sticky paste. "Good," Spider Woman said. "Now, Puukonhoya, smear that paste on the ladder rungs. Be careful!"

He smeared the berry paste over the rungs, and the sharp edges were blunted. Puukonhoya rushed up the ladder, with Spider Woman on his ear and Mole hiding in his hair, and entered Kwataka's lair. "There's his flint-arrowhead shirt!"

"Softly!" Spider Woman warned. "Kwataka is home, asleep in another room. I will cast a spell to keep him from hearing you, but you must still be careful!"

Puukonhoya quickly switched the real flint-arrowhead shirt with the counterfeit, slipping on the real shirt. He stole into the next room, and there was Lakone Mana, her hands and feet bound. Her eyes flashed with joy and alarm, and she whispered, "You mustn't stay! He kills anyone who enters!"

"I'm not leaving without you," Puukonhoya said, and cut her bonds.

But even though they were trying to be quiet, even though Spider Woman had cast that spell to keep Kwataka from hearing them, the Man-Eagle woke—and found himself facing Puukonhoya. "Who are you?" Kwataka asked sharply. "What are you doing here?"

"I am Puukonhoya, and I've come to rescue my wife!"

"Maybe you have and maybe you haven't," Kwataka snapped. "First you must win her from me. You must win a smoking contest with me. Do you see this tobacco pouch? We will both smoke, and the first to faint loses. If I lose, you may take back your wife. If I win, you die!"

"That tobacco is poisonous to humans," Spider Woman whispered in Puukonhoya's ear, "and Kwataka knows it. Mole, dig us a hole, if you would."

Mole dug a hole right where Puukonhoya stood, an air hole to the outside world so that when the young man took his turn at the smoking pipe, fresh air kept his head clear. Kwataka had no such air hole, and so it was he who nearly fainted. Hastily, the Man-Eagle hurried outside to clear his head. How had the human managed that? How had the human won?

"So you won the first contest," Kwataka snarled. "But that was only the first. There must be three."

Puukonhoya sighed. "If there must, there must. What is the second contest?"

"A simple thing," Kwataka said. "We shall each take up one of these great elk antlers. He who can break his antler with one snap wins."

"This is a trick," Spider Woman said to herself, and scuttled down to study the antlers.

Sure enough, the one intended for Kwataka was half-rotten, ready to fall apart at a touch, while the one meant for Puukonhoya was hard as stone. Spider Woman switched the two, so quickly and magically that Kwataka never suspected it. He snatched up what he thought was his antler—and nearly tore his arms from their sockets trying to break it. Puukonhoya snapped the half-rotten antler with one slight twist of his hands.

Kwataka stared. How had the human done that? "Very well," the Man-Eagle muttered, "you have won the second contest. But the third remains!"

"What is the third contest?" Puukonhoya asked.

"Do you see those two trees? Well, we both shall try to uproot them, leaves, branches, trunks and all. The one who can lift his tree free wins. The tree on the left is mine," he added, picking the one that had the shallowest roots.

Spider Woman whispered to Mole, "Loosen the roots of the tree on the right. Hurry!"

Mole hurried. He did such a fine job that when Puukonhoya pulled, the tree came up almost easily. Kwataka, meanwhile, found that even shallow roots could still be strong. He could hardly budge his tree at all.

"I win," Puukonhoya panted. "Now let my wife go."

"Not so fast, not so fast!" Kwataka cried. "I am hungry after all this work, and so, I guess, are you. That shall be the final contest. Yes, the fourth contest will be it! We shall both eat, and whichever eats the most, wins!"

"Hurry," Spider Woman whispered to Mole, "dig a hole next to Puukonhoya!"

Puukonhoya did eat some of the food, since he really *was* hungry, but the rest of it he let fall into the hole, bit by bit, till his plate was clean. Kwataka never guessed a thing. At last, too full to eat another bite, he said, "Enough!"

"Can't eat any more?" Puukonhoya asked. "Now I'll take my wife and—"

"Not so fast!" Kwataka cried. "One last test, one last test! Which of us is invulnerable, eh? Which of us can stand in a fire unscathed?"

He gathered two great piles of wood. Kwataka sat on one, Puukonhoya on the other. "Now your wife can light them," the Man-Eagle said, "and we shall see who survives this!"

Nervously, Lakone Mana lit the fires. But of course Puukonhoya was wearing the magical flint-arrowhead shirt, while Kwataka had only the counterfeit. The magical shirt produced ice to keep Puukonhoya nicely cool, but the resin shirt burned up in a flash, and Kwataka burned with it.

"Quickly," Spider Woman said to Puukonhoya, "take this magical cornmeal in your mouth and blow it all over Kwataka's ashes."

Puukonhoya obeyed. And a handsome man rose from the ashes. Spider Woman turned back into her woman-form and scolded him. "Have you learned your lesson? Have you?"

"I have," he who'd been Kwataka murmured like a little boy being scolded by his grandmother.

"Will you swear to stop killing people? Will you swear to stop carrying them off and eating them? Well? Will you swear that?"

"I swear it. I will never do evil deeds again."

"Then that's that," Spider Woman said in satisfaction. "Now we can all go home."

Asidenigan

A Magician from the Chippewa of Wisconsin

*N*o one knows the parentage of Asidenigan. There he was, a man living alone in the wilderness, one with his surroundings, living off the corn he raised and the beavers he trapped by his powers.

He might have gone on living like that, alone as a wild thing, and there would have been no tale about him, but Asidenigan was, after all, human. He grew lonely. So he hunted until he'd found a village, and went straight to the wigwam of the chief.

"I wish to stay here," he said.

The chief had heard stories about Asidenigan, the man who could catch beaver by magic. "You are welcome here," the chief said warmly. "You are very welcome."

But Asidenigan was watching the chief's daughter. He had never seen a woman, not in his lonely life, and the chief's daughter was, he thought, the most beautiful being he had ever seen.

"I wish to marry," he said. "I wish to marry *her*."

The young woman started at that. But Asidenigan was a fine-looking man, strong and lean from his life in the wilderness, and she thought to herself, "This is not such a bad thing."

The chief saw the looks the two were exchanging. This would be a fine way to keep Asidenigan in the tribe! "We cannot have any weddings," he said. "The people are too hungry. We have no meat here, and the meat-drying racks are bare."

"But there are plenty of beaver about!" Asidenigan said in surprise. "I will go hunting with your people."

Asidenigan joined the hunting party without a word. They were looking for beaver, so he strode right up to a beaver dam and tore it open. His power struck the beaver and they fell over like so many sticks. Carrying his prize back to the village, he dropped the beaver at the chief's feet.

"This is for you and your daughter. Now I will go back for food for the village."

Asidenigan made many trips into the wilderness, bringing back beaver and other food with each return. Soon all the wigwams had food in them, soon all the meat-drying racks were full. The winter was no hardship for the village now, and Asidenigan took the chief's daughter as his wife.

But the story does not end with this seemingly happy ending. Asidenigan was used to the wild places, the long silences. He was not used to being cooped up with people all around him. And with the coming of spring, he set out on longer and longer hunting expeditions, all alone.

Asidenigan's wife began to wonder if she'd wed too hastily. Yes, he was a fine-looking fellow, and kind to her. But he was so strange! "He is a beaver-man," she told herself, "a wild man who will never be a human being."

She ignored her younger sister, her younger sister who had loved Asidenigan from the moment she'd first seen him and who wept secretly because it was her sister, not she, who was Asidenigan's wife, and Asidenigan would not, not knowing the customs of the village, take a second wife.

Meanwhile, Asidenigan's wife was not the only one to wonder about this stranger they had admitted into their tribe. There are always people who will fear the newcomer, the different one, and Asidenigan, with his quietness and magic powers, made some of the tribe fearful. And what

people fear, they hate. Two young men from a neighboring
village stole into Asidenigan's wigwam when he was away
hunting, and no one noticed. They brought his wife a gift of
a partridge and whispered to her:

"The people have decided to slay the beaver-man. You
need have no fear; we have a handsome young man, a normal
man, for you to wed. But first we must kill Asidenigan. When
he returns, you must tell him nothing of this. We will come
and kill him in the night."

The wife hesitated only a short time. She wanted to be
rid of this strange husband of hers! "I will tell him nothing,"
she agreed.

But when Asidenigan returned, he saw the footprints
outside his wigwam, not the clear steps of an honest visitor
or two, but the sly, half-erased prints of someone trying to
hide a visit. He entered, and his wife greeted him as though
nothing was wrong. But Asidenigan glanced at his war club,
and his powers told him: "Four eyes have looked at this
today."

"Impossible," his wife said. "No one has been here but
me."

But Asidenigan saw the partridge she was cooking.
"Where did you get that bird?"

"Oh, it was a gift from some hunters."

"These hunters plan to kill me."

This was his magical power speaking. Asidenigan's wife
cringed back in alarm, but she insisted, "No, no, no one wants
to kill you."

"They will come for me tonight. When they do," he
added, taking down his war club, "you must hold fast to my
belt and you will be safe."

The one blindness of Asidenigan was that he refused to
see how his wife hated him; he would not believe she had
turned against him.

The night came, and with it, came the warriors. They were expecting Asidenigan to be asleep. They were not expecting a wide-awake warrior in full battle rage! Asidenigan killed several of his attackers before they could strike and would have killed them all. But his wife let go of her grip on his belt, and the remaining men carried her off into the night. Asidenigan, too weary from his fight against many to pursue them, sank bitterly to the ground, aching with sorrow over his wife who had, he saw now, betrayed him.

But sorrow turned to anger.

"They feared my powers, did they? Now they shall see those powers unleashed!"

Asidenigan found himself some corn and meat to eat, to fuel his strength, feed his powers, then set out, fed and restored, to track the men who'd tried to kill him and who had stolen his wife. He saw the way as no man without powers could do, he followed close behind, finding where they had stopped to dance about a campfire, thinking themselves safe and Asidenigan far away. He followed to where another village stood, there on the far side of a lake, and listened to the sound of their dancing drift across the water to him.

"They are there, the ones who tried to kill me, the ones who stole my wife."

How could he cross? He had no boat, and it was too far to swim. Asidenigan snatched up a little wooden ball, an oak gall. Yes, this would do. He put the little ball in the water, then made himself shrink, shrink, shrink, till he could creep inside the wooden ball and let the wind carry it safely across the water.

Asidenigan crept out and grew, grew, grew back to his normal height, but made himself invisible as he did so. He stalked silently into the village, into one long wigwam where the men were dancing.

One man did not dance. He sat beside Asidenigan's wife, and it was clear enough that both were pleased with this arrangement. Asidenigan pointed, willing thirst into the man. The woman rose to get water for him, but the man sent two boys with her as a guard.

"Fools," Asidenigan snarled, and threw them both to the ground with terrible force.

His wife shook with terror. "Asidenigan? Is—is that you?"

He was still invisible. "Yes."

"I didn't want to go with them," she whimpered. "They made me go. Come, husband, come, let's go home."

"No. Pick up that pail. Fill it with water and take it inside. Hurry!"

She was too frightened to argue. But back inside the wigwam, the man beside whom she'd been sitting saw her fright and guessed at the truth.

"Build up the fires!" he cried. "Let them burn brightly!"

So brightly did they burn that Asidenigan's shadow was seen. The men captured him, too many seizing him for him to fight, and he let himself become visible.

"Now you will dance for us!" the men mocked.

"First I must eat," he said. "All that magic has made me hungry. Wife, will you give me some meat?"

Was Asidenigan still hoping, deep within him, that she loved him? But she, afraid of him and wanting to be rid of him, threw the meat, blazing right from the fire, at him. Asidenigan cried out in pain and, with a great burst of magic, flew from there, up and out through the smokehole, away and down into a hollow stump when he collapsed, safely sheltered but badly burned.

Time passed. Asidenigan's magic healed him and he returned to his father-in-law's village. There, he called a council and told everyone what had happened. His brother-in-law, an honest, honorable young man, was the most horrified of them all. "You must be avenged," he cried. "And I will help you."

"I will go alone."

"I will go with you!" the young man insisted. "It is my sister who betrayed you!"

So they left together, and several of the warriors went with them. The enemy village had been fortified, but Asidenigan and his band broke right through. He slew all those who had tried to slay him. But it was the brother-in-law who slew his wife. She who had tried to have her husband slain died there and then.

Asidenigan and the others returned to their village. But Asidenigan's heart was bitter, for now he was alone and would forever be lonely.

Would he? His brother-in-law said, "I have a second sister. She would be your wife."

This was the younger sister, the one who had secretly loved Asidenigan all this while. He saw no fear in her heart, no treachery. Asidenigan said to her, "I cannot live in a village, that I have learned."

She said, "I cannot live anywhere but with you."

And so Asidenigan wed her, and built her a fine home in the forest, and the two lived happily together all their days.

Glooscap

A Magician from the Wabanaki of New England and Canada

Glooscap was known to many people. Some called him Glooskap, others Kuloscap, but all agreed that he was a mighty magician. Indeed, he was more than a mere man and powerful enough to have made a good many things, including animals. Though he could play pranks when the fancy took him and make people laugh, Glooscap was a hero when the need arose.

And the need arose in the form of a family of giants, terrible Kiwa'kws, Ice Giants, who were cruel for the sake of cruelty. They committed horrible acts without a thought of regret and ate whatever people they could catch.

Glooscap heard about these terrible beings and sighed. "The Ice Giants are my distant kin. But they have turned to evil. And since they are eating people, they must be destroyed."

He could change his shape as easily as he could frame a thought. Glooscap saw that the old father of the Ice-Giants, the head of their clan, was grey-skinned and one-eyed. And instantly, Glooscap was that one's exact image. He went and sat down beside the old Ice-Giant, and all the others marvelled at the likeness. They had just enough politeness not to ask him any questions. And one of the Ice-Giant women even brought him some whale meat.

But another of the Ice-Giants shouted, "This stranger eats too well!" and ran off with the meat.

"I'll get that meat back," Glooscap said. Closing his eyes, he wished the whale meat back to him—and back it came.

Now the Ice-Giants knew that a magician had come into their midst. "But how powerful is he?" they wondered. "We must test him."

So the strongest of the Ice-Giants brought the great jawbone of a whale. He tried to break it, but for all his strength, he could barely bend the tough bone. But Glooscap broke it with a flash of his magic, broke the jawbone as though it was a rotten twig.

The Ice-Giants muttered together. "We must test him further," they decided.

So they brought a great pipe and filled it with tobacco, magic tobacco that would kill anyone who wasn't truly powerful. "Come into the smoke-hut," they said, and once inside, handed Glooscap the pipe. All of them watched as he began to smoke it, clearly hoping to see him be slain.

Glooscap, however, smoked it without any trouble. But when he tried to pass the pipe back to the Ice-Giants, they refused it.

"Not yet, not yet. Let us smoke some more."

"So now," Glooscap thought, "they are beginning to fear me. They're going to try killing me. They will learn I'm not so easy to kill!"

Sure enough, the Ice-Giants had secretly sealed up the smoke-hut. No air could get in; no smoke could get out. But Glooscap's magic found tiny airholes in the walls of the hut, enough to let him breathe.

The Ice-Giants had no such magic. They ran gasping for air from the hut. Glooscap followed calmly. The Ice-Giants glared at him, but all they said was, "Let us play a game of ball."

"I can imagine the ballgame you'd play," Glooscap said. "You'd love to play it with my head. So I shall provide the ball. And a head you shall have!"

He conjured a skull, a hideous Ice-Giant skull, so hideous that the Ice-Giants cried out in fear. This magician was far too powerful for them! They turned and fled.

But Glooscap was not going to let them escape to work their harm elsewhere. He stamped his foot so fiercely that all the earth echoed and water gushed down from the mountains. The Ice-Giants were caught in the flood and turned into fish. As fish they remained, unable to work any harm on anyone again.

But Glooscap went on to further adventures. There was a village of cats, black cats, and Glooscap took on the shape and style of Pogumk, chief of the village. He lived among the cat- people for a time, though why he did this is known only to Glooscap. Perhaps he was weary from his deeds, or bored with humankind. Or maybe it was because he had already recognized that another of the villagers wasn't a true cat, either. She was Pukjinskwes, a being who could, in addition to turning into a cat, be man or woman as he or she wished.

And it had been in woman form that Pukjinskwes had taken a fancy to Glooscap. Back then, he had scorned her, fled from her, and her love had turned to hate. Now, transformed into a cat, she hated Pogumk and plotted to be chief in his place. Pretending innocence, she said to Pogumk, "Let us take a canoe and gather duck eggs."

But when Pogumk went ashore onto an island, Pukjinskwes paddled off and left him stranded. "He will never find his way back," she thought. "He will starve where he stands."

Back at the village, Pukjinskwes told all the cat-people, "Pogumk has abandoned us. I am chief now!"

No one wanted to believe her. They searched all through the forest and over the rivers and lakes looking for Pogumk.

But when they couldn't find him, they sadly agreed that he was gone. "Pukjinskwes shall be our new chief."

Meanwhile, Pogumk was searching for a way off the island. He couldn't swim well in cat-form. Of course, he could have changed back to Glooscap and magicked himself over the water. But maybe he didn't want Pukjinskwes to learn who he truly was. Instead, Pogumk began to sing. He sang in a magical fashion, calling to Fox, a magician-friend of his. He sang so that the song reached Fox, far away.

"My friend is in trouble," Fox said, and set out to find him.

There Pogumk was, trapped on the island. Fox swam easily across and said, "Take my tail. I will tow you back to the mainland."

But it was not to be quite that simple. Pukjinskwes, seeing from afar what they were doing, conjured a storm to stop them. Pogumk and Fox nearly drowned, but after a struggle that took them nearly all the day and all the night, they reached the far bank and lay there panting.

At last Pogumk got to his feet. "I must see what's become of the people," he told Fox.

But the people had moved on; their campfire was quite cold. Pogumk pursued, and at last overcame his family (or perhaps, since he was really Glooscap in cat-person form, his adopted family). They were overjoyed to see him, since Pukjinskwes had assured everyone he was dead.

"I live," said Pogumk, "and now I shall rid you of Pukjinskwes. Go and steal away her baby," he told his foster brother, Sable, "and cast it into the fire."

Was this a true baby? Was it merely a thing conjured by Pukjinskwes as Pukjinskwes conjured male or female shape? At any rate, into the fire it went, and Pukjinskwes came roaring with rage, hunting Pogumk.

"No need to hunt," he said, stepping out from behind a tree. "Here I am."

She shrieked and charged, but he, bringing forth Glooscap's power, threw her back against a tree. And there she stuck. All night she stuck. But Pukjinskwes had with her a stone axe, and for all of the next day she hacked and hewed awkwardly behind her till at last she was free. She went shrieking after the cat- people.

But Pukjinskwes hadn't been able to remove all the bark. Bits and pieces still stuck all over her, making her look not like a terrible being to be feared but like one to make people laugh. And laugh they did, till at last Pukjinskwes fled, raging and full of shame. She sat down far from any sign of any people at all, muttering and swearing to herself.

"I wish," she said at last, "I wish that I could become something to torment everyone!"

And with that, Pukjinskwes became the first mosquito. Later, she turned back into her true monstrous self, but her mosquito form remained and multiplied. Pukjinskwes, sure that Pogumk, that Glooscap, was watching, never dared let herself be seen by daylight again. She lurked in the darkness, and there she still lurks. But as long as there is light of any fashion, Pukjinskwes, for fear of Glooscap, dares not approach.

Asin

A Magician from the Toba of Argentina

*A*sin appeared out of nowhere one day and walked right up to the house of a pretty young woman, who was the daughter of Chief Nalarate. But Asin was hardly a pretty sight just then. No, he looked like nothing more than a hairless, potbellied little boy. And when Nalarate saw him, he said, "What are you doing here, ugly thing? Did you think you could steal from me?"

"I have no intention of turning thief," Asin told him calmly. "I have merely come to borrow a comb from your daughter."

"A comb!" Nalarate sneered. "What could such a hairless little worm as you want with a comb?"

"Hairless or no," Asin said, "I would like to comb myself."

Nalarate's daughter overheard, and felt pity for this odd, ugly little boy. "I will lend you a comb," she told him.

Asin thanked her, took the comb, and went off to the nearby lagoon. Now Nalarate's daughter was consumed with curiosity. "How," she wondered, "can a hairless boy comb himself?"

So she took up a jar and set off for the lagoon as though merely getting water for the family. But once the young woman had reached the lagoon, she stepped off the path and hid in the bushes.

Ah, and what a marvel she saw! The ugly, hairless little potbellied boy had turned into a handsome young man bathing in the lagoon, his long black hair floating like a cloak about his head. Nalarate's daughter stared and never doubted that this was a true magician. But she also knew in that moment that she had just fallen utterly in love. This was the man she wished to marry.

The young man slipped easily out of the water and began to comb out his long hair. He dressed, then, passing both hands over his face and hair, became the ugly, hairless, potbellied little boy once more.

"So be it," Nalarate's daughter murmured. If her parents learned that she wanted to marry the ugly little boy, they would be horrified and try to forbid it. "They shall not know the truth," she decided.

She quickly filled the water jug and hurried home. The mysterious little boy had come and gone and left her comb, but Nalarate's daughter knew he would return.

And so he did the next day. Nalarate's daughter invited him into her father's house, then sat beside him. "I wish to marry you," she said.

"You do? But I am just an ugly little boy!"

"I love you, ugly little boy, and I'll marry you even if my parents forbid it."

"You don't feel any disgust at the sight of me?" he asked as though he didn't quite believe it.

"None. You see, my love, I know you as you truly are."

They went outside, sitting happily together. Everyone who saw them laughed. "Such a pretty woman wasted on such an ugly boy!"

Nalarate came storming up. "What do you think you're doing?" he shouted at his daughter. "Leave that ugly thing!"

"No. This is my husband." That was all the marriage ceremony her people used.

"But how will he hunt, such a useless thing? How can he provide you with food?"

"I will," Asin said quietly.

That night, Asin and his new wife went to sleep in each other's arms. When the young woman woke, she found herself surrounded by everything one of her people could want: all manner of cloth and food, even a fine new mosquito net.

"I think I like being married to a magician!" she said, stroking her handsome husband's long hair, and grinned.

When the young woman's mother saw how happy her daughter had become, she made a point of learning about Asin, of talking to him and listening to what he had to say. And a strong friendship sprang up between the two.

"Whatever you wish," Asin told her, "just ask. I can provide for you as easily as I provide for my dear wife."

"I believe it. But," she asked, teasing this proud young magician, "what do I wish right now?"

Asin smiled. "I know." He reached under his sleeping mat and pulled out a fine honeycomb. "There is not a single bee in this, either, just plenty of rich, sweet honey."

"Just like my husband," his wife purred. And for that, Asin gave her a length of fine blue cloth.

Meanwhile, Nalarate was growing more and more jealous. He refused to admit that Asin was truly powerful. He told everyone that what Asin did were tricks, nothing but tricks. Every day Nalarate spent more and more time drinking algarrobo beer with the warriors. Every day he said worse and worse things about Asin.

"Mother, what are we going to do?" the young wife asked. "Father is very angry. He may even try to take our clothes away!" That was how a man declared a divorce; he took back all he gifts he had given his wife. But for Nalarate to try that would have been nothing less than theft!

"Never mind," Asin soothed. "That's not important right now. Nalarate has been spending too much time with the warriors, the bored warriors. Now my spirit tells me that he is planning a war campaign."

Sure enough, Nalarate, staggering a little from the beer he had drunk, returned announcing, "I am going to war. But," he added, "I will *not* take your husband along, daughter. I don't like him. He's too ugly to make a warrior!" Nalarate had never seen Asin in his true shape. "He's too poor; he doesn't even have a horse. He's useless!"

Asin said nothing. But afterwards he told his wife, "I will join the war party. But don't tell this to your father."

As the war party, all mounted on their swift horses, rode out, Nalarate commanded that each warrior ride by his daughter. She was to look at each in turn and decide which should be her husband. Nalarate's daughter didn't waste time insisting that she was already wed. Instead, she obediently looked at each warrior as he rode by, but said nothing. Last in line was Asin, in his ugly little potbellied boy guise, riding on a donkey.

"Here is my husband," Nalarate's daughter cried.

All the warriors burst into mocking laughter. "That? That ugly little thing? He can't hunt or fight!"

Nalarate was so furious that he shouted, "Then my daughter starves! For I shall give her nothing!"

"If I have my husband," the young woman cried, "then I shall want for nothing!"

The war party rode out. Nalarate set a rapid pace, sure that Asin and his poor little donkey would be left in the dust. But as soon as all the warriors were out of sight, Asin changed the donkey to a magical horse, and easily caught up. Some warriors laughed, others wondered, and still others pitied the ugly little boy.

"He has courage," they murmured. "Whatever else he may lack, Asin has courage."

And they slipped him bits of meat, afraid that he would starve along the way. Asin took the meat like the starving little boy he was pretending to be, and said nothing.

Then the war party sighted the enemy. "Stay back," Nalarate snapped at Asin. "We're about to fight."

"I know."

"They have weapons!"

"I know."

"Stay back! That's an order!"

With that, Nalarate and his war party charged forward, leaving Asin and his donkey in the dust. But Asin quickly changed to his handsome self, clad in warrior's garb. Changing his donkey to the magical horse, he charged the foe, entered their camp, and came away with many horses, magically attracted to him, and much honor.

"Who is that?" Nalarate asked. "Who is that?"

"I am Asin!" Asin cried. "I am your daughter's husband!"

And he quickly rode out of sight, hurrying back to his wife and her mother. "We must leave before Nalarate returns. He will try to kill me in his rage, and he might harm you." He glanced at his mother-in-law. "What of you? We are friends. Will you come, too?"

"Yes. Nalarate has not been a kind husband to me. I will, indeed."

Off they went. Nalarate arrived to find his wife and daughter gone and his house empty. "What have you done?" his warriors cried. "That was a magician your daughter wed. Did you not know? Did you not see?"

"I saw only an ugly little potbellied boy!" Nalarate cried. "What else was there to see?"

But many of his warriors were too disgusted by what they saw as his bad judgement to stay with him. They went after Asin and said, "Let us join you."

Nalarate, with his forces reduced to just a few warriors, decided to make one last attempt to be rid of Asin. Asin, Nalarate thought, would surely be resting after all his labors, he and those who had followed him. They would not be expecting an attack.

But Nalarate, camped by the edge of a lagoon, didn't know that Asin was on the other side. Asin stretched out his hand over the water, and those warriors who were in any way touching it fell dead in an instant. Nalarate was left alone and dejected.

But Asin and his family and his new tribe fared well from then on.

Setna and Se-Osiris

Two Magicians from Ancient Egypt

Setna and his young son, Se-Osiris, were said to be the two greatest magicians in all of Egypt in the days of the Pharaohs. Setna, it was said, had even read the mighty Book of Thoth, god of Wisdom, and knew every spell within it, and had taught his son to be just as learned. And whenever Pharaoh was faced with a problem that could not be solved by ordinary human means, he would send for the two magicians.

As he did this day. For an ambassador from Nubia, the land to Egypt's south, had arrived at court, a tall, menacing man who looked more as though he came in war as in peace. "I have come," he announced after scarce courtesies had been completed, "to declare the magics of Nubia far mightier than those of Egypt."

Now this, Pharaoh realized, was as good as a declaration of war, so he quickly sent messengers to Setna—

Being the magician he was, he had already arrived in the council hall, together with his son. Setna was tall and handsome, with wise, dark eyes that had seen many strange wonders. Se-Osiris was still barely more than a boy, and one might laugh to think of him as a magician—until one saw the same strange wisdom in his eyes. Se-Osiris had inherited every bit of his father's powers.

"Are *these* your mightiest magicians?" the Nubian ambassador said scornfully.

"We are competent enough," Setna said calmly.

"So be it! Then you will have no problem in reading the message that is on this sealed papyrus scroll—without," he added with a narrow smile, "breaking the seal."

Not by the slightest twitch of a muscle did Setna show his reaction. "My son is more skilled in that art than I."

"I shall do the reading," Se-Osiris agreed quietly.

"You?" the Nubian laughed. "A mere boy? Well, well, well, the magics of Egypt are weak indeed!"

"They are not," Se-Osiris said, and his gaze grew misty and strange as he began his magic. "The scroll tells of a great insult done to a Pharaoh five hundred years ago."

This time it was the Nubian ambassador who showed not the slightest twitch of a muscle. "Does it? Go on, boy. What else does this sealed scroll state?"

"There was a gathering of magicians," Se-Osiris continued, "Egyptian and Nubian both. And as happens when men are gathered together, the magicians began to boast. One claimed that he could darken the world for three days. Another added that he could bring down a drought upon the land. But a third magician, a Nubian, stated boldly: "'I could cast a compulsion over Pharaoh himself that would bring him helplessly to Nubia for a beating—'"

At those words, a great roar of anger went up from the assembled courtiers. Setna held up a warning hand. "Do not break my son's concentration. Continue, Se-Osiris."

And the boy, his dreamy gaze never wavering, continued, "'— for a beating. Then,' the magician claimed, 'I would bring him back again to his palace, all within the space of half a day.'"

Se-Osiris paused. "Is this not truly what is written on the scroll?"

"So far," the Nubian grudgingly admitted. "So far. But there is more. Can you read the rest?"

Without hesitation, the boy continued, "When Pharaoh heard these bold words, he laughed. 'If you can do this to me,' he told the Nubian magician, 'then I will proclaim you the greatest magician in the Two Lands.'

"Alas, it happened just as the Nubian magician had stated. Pharaoh was, indeed, magicked away to Nubia and beaten there like a common slave."

Again the courtiers shouted out in rage. Again Setna held up a warning hand. And Se-Osiris continued, "After that, all of Pharaoh's magicians gathered together and worked their strongest spells. And they brought the King of Nubia before Pharaoh and had *him* beaten in turn. So furious was the King of Nubia that he should have suffered for his magician's boast and that the two magics of Egypt and Nubia had not won, one over the other, that he said to that magician with the full fury of the gods behind him: "'May you wander the Two Lands in endless life till the day you can prove one land's magic the greater.'"

Se-Osiris stopped, arms folded. "Is that not what the scroll says?"

In answer, the Nubian cast it down. A scribe hurriedly picked up the scroll, broke the seal and read it. "Yes," he assured everyone eagerly. "That is exactly what is written here."

"And I think I know who that ageless magician may be," Setna added quietly. "You are he," he said to the Nubian ambassador." And you have come to settle the magical war between our two lands."

"I have, indeed!" the Nubian magician cried.

And suddenly—oh, terrible! A great cobra reared up before Pharaoh, ready to strike!

But Setna pointed, and the snake became a harmless worm. Se-Osiris quickly crushed it beneath his sandal. The Nubian magician laughed harshly and brought darkness down over the court.

But Setna reached out and pulled the darkness to him, rolling it up as a child rolls up a ball of twine. The Nubian magician shouted in rage, and a great wall of flame sprang up.

But Setna cried out a commanding Word of Power. The flame curled back upon the Nubian magician, and in a moment, that ancient being had turned to ash.

The battle was ended. And no magical war was ever again fought in those lands.

Mbokothe

A Magician from the Akamba of Kenya

Mbokothe and his younger brother were orphans, poor boys with barely enough to eat and only two scrawny cows as property. One day Mbokothe told his brother, "We can no longer live like this, never knowing if the next day will bring starvation. I will take our two cows to a wise man, a medicine man, and see if I can't barter them for magical powers."

"But what if the medicine man refuses?"

"Then we shall be no worse off than we are now!" Mbokothe declared.

And off he went, driving the two cows before him. It was a long journey and a wearying one, but at last Mbokothe had arrived at the home of the great medicine man. Mbokothe was almost too dry and tired by that time to speak, but the medicine man gave him water and said, "I know why you've come. Two cows aren't enough to buy all my knowledge. But I will teach you this one magic power for the price of the cows: I will teach you how to transform yourself into whatever you please. Be careful with this power," he added. "Be careful not to play one trick too many."

Mbokothe agreed that he would be careful. And so the medicine man taught him the magic of transformation, and sent him home. It can only be imagined how Mbokothe played with his new power, turning himself to animal and bird and back again.

But when he reached his home, Mbokothe forgot all his games. His brother was sitting sadly in the dust, all but starving.

"I will get us wealth," Mbokothe promised. "But first you must promise never to tell anyone that I can turn myself into animals and birds."

His brother promised. Mbokothe turned himself into a fine black bull and his brother took him to market to sell. Everyone was amazed at the sight of so splendid and powerful a bull, and one man asked Mbokothe's brother, "What do you want for this beast?"

Mbokothe had already told his brother what to say. "I want two fat cows and five fat goats."

This was a good price, a high price, but the man, looking at the splendid bull, its black hide gleaming in the sunlight sighed and said, "Agreed."

He gave Mbokothe's brother the two fat cows and five fat goats, and the boy began driving them home. Meanwhile, the man began driving the great black bull. But suddenly the bull turned and threatened him with its horns, then thundered off into the underbrush. The man ran after it with all his strength, but could not keep up. At last, panting and exhausted, he had to slow to a walk.

But Mbokothe had turned himself into a lion and trampled over the tracks he had left as a bull. When the man reached this spot, he cried, "The bull has already been eaten by a lion!" Disgusted with his bad luck, he went home.

Mbokothe turned back into himself. Grinning, he returned to his home, where his brother was waiting with the two fat cows and five fat goats. "I told you I would get us wealth!" Mbokothe said.

"We are fine now," his brother said. "We don't need any more."

"This is not enough," Mbokothe said. "I want to be sure we don't starve again."

So he turned back into a bull and had his brother take him to another market. Again, Mbokothe's brother sold him for a fine price in cows and goats, again he escaped his buyer and went home.

"Now we don't have to worry," Mbokothe's brother said. "Now we are wealthy in cows and goats. There is no need for you to risk yourself again."

But Mbokothe said, "One more time. Just one more time."

So he turned himself into a bull and had his brother take him to yet another market. Sure enough, Mbokothe's brother sold him for a fine price, and sure enough, he escaped his buyer yet again.

But this time, Mbokothe thought, instead of making it look as though a lion had eaten the bull, this time it would be fun to frighten away the man as well.

Alas, what Mbokothe didn't know was that this time the man who had bought the "bull" was also a magician. So when Mbokothe turned himself into a lion, the man turned himself into a larger, fiercer lion. Mbokothe turned to run, and the magician chased him.

He was gaining on Mbokothe! He was going to catch Mbokothe!

So Mbokothe turned into a bird and quickly took to the air. But the magician turned to a bird as well and chased him!

Mbokothe landed and turned to an antelope bounding off across the plain. But the magician turned to an antelope, too, and chased him! They ran and they ran until at last Mbokothe could run no more. He collapsed in a heap, and the magician collapsed beside him.

They both turned back into their rightful shapes. "That was a fine chase," Mbokothe said at last. "But you win."

"I know. Mbokothe, I knew you were a magician from the moment I first saw you in the form of a bull. I could have killed you then or now, but I didn't. Do you know why?"

"You want your goats back?"

"Of course I do. I wanted to teach you a lesson, boy. Though you are a fine magician, there will always be someone more powerful than you. Do you understand me?"

"I do," Mbokothe said.

He gave the magician back his goats. From that day on, Mbokothe was always careful not to misuse his powers. He knew that there was always going to be someone more powerful than he!

Elephant Girl

Two Magicians from the Ju/'hoan of Botswana

$\mathcal{J}$his story takes place in the long-ago days when shapes were still fluid and changeable. And so Elephant Girl could be born with ties both to her human mother and the elephant folk. But it was with her human grandmother that she held the strongest tie, that of love.

That grandmother had powers not known to most folk. Where she'd learned them, who had taught her—no one knew. But they were good powers that helped her people find food, so no one worried about them.

Elephant Girl grew to be a woman, and was married, as was the custom, to a young man of another clan. He lived with her people for a time, then said, "I miss my own clan. I'll visit them, and return here with gifts for you, my wife."

He reached his home without trouble, and had a happy reunion with his family, especially with his mother, who was nearly ready to give birth.

"When you go back to your wife," she said with a smile, "your baby brother or sister shall stay here to keep me company."

But when the young man was ready to leave, the baby leaped from his mother's womb, growing into a boy, and then a man, as everyone stared in shock.

"This is surely not a human child!" they gasped. "Here is surely a child of Glara!" That was the trickster-god, he with his wily, magical ways. A child of his would be a strange one, indeed!

But this was something far, far worse.

"I will go with my brother," the newly-born man declared.

No one dared to argue.

Off the two brothers went to Elephant Girl's people. Her husband said nothing about his brother's sudden birth and growth, and no one suspected anything—no one except for Elephant Girl and her grandmother. But what could they say? The newly-grown brother acted with polite, proper courtesy. They could not accuse him of anything! And the two brothers had brought splendid gifts.

"Pack up your belongings, Elephant Girl," her husband said. "Now you must visit my family."

"I don't want to go," Elephant Girl whispered to her grandmother. "Something is very wrong."

But then magic stirred between the two women. They both knew in that moment what would happen, what could not be changed—and what could and would. Grimly, Elephant Girl went with her husband and brother. The younger brother secretly took off his sandals and hurled them away. "Turn to vultures!" he whispered to them.

And they became two vultures.

"Look!" the younger brother cried. "Where there are vultures, there is meat! There's no need for us to go home empty-handed. Come, brother, let's go hunting!"

He pretended to run, then stumbled and cried out, "Ow! Ow! I have a thorn in my foot! You go on without me. Elephant Girl, help me get this stupid thorn out of my foot so I can help my brother."

Elephant Girl took out her awl, her long, strong bone needle, then stopped. "I don't see any thorn."

"Oh, it's gone in too deeply. Here, give me the awl. I'll do it myself."

Elephant Girl gave him the awl. And he stabbed her with it, and killed her.

Now this was exactly what Elephant Girl and her grandmother had known would happen. And, as they had known it would, a small wind caught up a few drops of her blood and carried it safely to her grandmother. That wise woman hid the drops of blood in a small bottle.

"My poor granddaughter has been killed," she said to herself. "But that is not the end of it."

Meanwhile, the older brother, Elephant Girl's husband, had failed to find any meat. The vultures had, though he didn't know it, turned back into sandals. But when he returned to camp, there was meat! His younger brother was sitting by a fire and peacefully eating. He grinned. "Come and join me."

"What meat is that?"

"Oh, this, this is antelope, an eland."

"It doesn't look like eland to me. And where is Elephant Girl? Where is my wife?"

"She ran off."

"Did she? Did she? Younger brother, what is that meat?"

"It's nothing but an eland, I told you that, a foolish eland that let me stab it. Come, eat."

At last the older brother ate. They brought the meat home, and everyone ate. And no one asked about Elephant Girl.

Meanwhile, Elephant Girl's grandmother was working secret magic over the drops of blood. They began to grow. The wise woman transferred them to a skin bag and continued her magic. Soon the skin bag was too small. She transferred the blood to a larger bag, and then a larger one yet, and all the time kept working her secret magic. And when she was done—there was Elephant Girl alive again.

"My husband's brother murdered me. Both brothers ate me. My husband did not refuse to eat. He did not even try to find me."

"Wait," her grandmother said. "We are not yet done."

Sure enough, one day the two brothers came into the camp. They saw Elephant Girl and stopped short, staring.

"How could she be alive?" the younger brother wondered, but only to himself. He dared not say anything.

The older brother was frightened, too. He had known, deep within him, that it hadn't been an eland he'd eaten, but his wife. But what could he say? "Will you come home with me, Elephant Girl?"

"I will."

But the wise grandmother secretly gave her a gemsbok horn. "When you are in your husband's camp," she whispered, "blow this horn. And justice will be done."

Elephant Girl took the horn. She went with her husband and his brother to their people's camp. There, she blew the horn, the magical gemsbok horn. Three times she blew. The first blast slew her husband who had eaten her. The second blast slew any in the camp who'd tasted the meat. And the third and final blast slew that evil younger brother.

"Justice has been done," Elephant Girl said, and went back to her people.

Clever Aja

A Magician from the Ashante of Ghana

nce a woman gave birth to not one, not two, but seven children, seven boys, at one time. Amazing, that—but more amazing still was the boy born last, the seventh son, Aja. For Aja was born with powers all his own, and with a magical cowtail switch in his hand.

Some years later, when the babies had become children, the chief learned of this amazing seven-sons-at-a-time birth and decided that this could be no good omen. *These unnatural boys,* he thought, *must die!* So he ordered them to cut seven sticks from the forest. There, the chief planted a deadly trap.

Aja, clever youngster that he was, suspected that trap. "I, Aja, say that this wood should become seven sticks," he proclaimed, and struck a tree with his cowtail switch. Instantly, the tree became seven smooth sticks.

When the chief saw the sticks, so perfectly smooth and even, he knew they could not have been cut so quickly without magic. And how else but by magic could the seven boys have escaped his trap? And who else, he thought, seeing Aja staring right back at him, could have worked that magic but this seventh son, this Aja?

"I have a task for you," the chief said to Aja. "You must go to the home of Death and bring back his snuff bottle, his grinding stone and his flyswitch."

If Aja refused, the chief thought, he would be put to death. If Aja accepted, well then, he probably would never return. Either way, the chief thought, he would be rid of the young magician. And with Aja gone, the remaining six boys could easily be put to death.

"I will go," Aja said, "and bring back Death's snuff bottle, his grinding stone and his flyswitch."

Off he went, taking with him some bread and fish.

No sooner was Aja out of sight than the chief had his six brothers slain and buried. There they lay, and there they must stay for now.

Meanwhile, as Aja crossed a stream, the stream spoke: "I'm hungry. Feed me and I will help you."

"Of course," Aja said, and gave the stream some of his bread and fish.

He came to a tree. And it said, "I'm hungry. Feed me and I will help you."

"Of course," Aja said, and gave the tree some of his bread and fish.

Now he had only a little food left. But when a fly said, "I'm hungry. Feed me and I will help you," Aja knew better than to refuse. "Of course," he said, and gave the fly the last of his bread and fish.

Aja travelled on. And at last he came to Death's house. Death looked at him in surprise. "Not many living men come to me. But you are welcome here. Come, spend the night as my guest."

Aja knew that a being as powerful as Death was not going to change his nature; Death would surely try to kill this living visitor. So when Death asked, "Have you any secrets?" Aja was prepared.

"Indeed," he said with a smile. "I only snore when I'm awake."

Aja's brothers had once told him that he snored quite loudly when he slept. Now Aja was able to go peacefully to sleep. Every time Death checked to see if the boy was asleep, the sound of snoring would stop him. At last, frustrated, Death cried, "Why are you not sleeping?"

Aja came instantly awake. "I can't sleep because I have a terrible headache. So terrible is it that only one thing could help me sleep: snuff."

So Death gave Aja his snuff bottle. Aja settled back to sleep and soon was snoring away like thunder. Death cried, "Why are you still not sleeping?"

"I can't sleep because there's a very noisy fly buzzing about my face. If I had a flyswitch, I could slap it and get some sleep."

So Death gave Aja his flyswitch. Aja settled back to sleep and soon was snoring away like an earthquake. Death cried, *"Now* why are you not sleeping?"

"I can't sleep because a whole troop of ants are crawling up the wall. If I had a grinding stone, I could grind them up and get some sleep."

So Death gave Aja his grinding stone. By now it was nearly morning. If Death didn't kill Aja now, he would have to wait till the next night! And Death didn't want to wait.

But just as Death was about to kill Aja, Aja cried, "Fly, fly, I fed you! Now aid me!"

And the fly Aja had fed bit Death sharply on the neck. Death yelped with surprise, and Aja ran for his life. But here came Death right behind him!

"Tree, tree, I fed you!" Aja cried. "Now aid me!"

And the tree Aja had fed loomed large in Death's path, blocking him. But Death cut his way through. And he came again, running after Aja.

"Stream, stream, I fed you!" Aja cried. "Now aid me!"

The stream flooded. Death was left stranded where he was. And Aja escaped.

But as Aja neared the chief's encampment, he saw the six graves of his brothers. "So that's what the chief was doing while I was away," Aja said. And with six waves of his cowtail switch, he woke them from their deadly sleep.

The chief was astonished, of course, to learn of Aja's return. But he was not yet ready to give up. Instead he sent for a powerful magician, a fetish priest. Aja wasn't at all sure his own magic was up to this challenge, so he told his brothers, "We'll all hide in the top of this tree."

So up the boys climbed. But the fetish magician was a clever one. He learned the seven boys' names and called them one by one, each time saying, "Come down to me." And each time he called, another boy fell from the tree to the ground far below, fell down dead once more.

When it came to Aja's turn, the boy plucked a leaf and named it "Aja" after him. And when the fetish priest called his name, Aja told the leaf, "It's you he calls."

The leaf fell. But the fetish priest realized Aja's trick and quickly called his name again. This time Aja told a leaf, "We both must fall this time."

The leaf cushioned his fall, and Aja hid under it. This time the fetish priest was fooled. He went on making magic, pulling every leaf off the tree, trying to find Aja. At last, furious, he climbed the tree, determined to pull the boy down by hand.

While he was doing that, the fetish priest left his box of magic unguarded. Aja snatched it up and cried, "Now *you* must fall!"

The fetish priest fell, fell to his death.

Aja, opening the magic box, found a leaf to return the dead to life. He touched each of his brothers in turn, and each came back to life. So happy was Aja to see them that he threw the leaf aside without thinking. It landed on the fetish priest—and *he* came back to life.

"I don't want to fight you any more," he told Aja. "We are too evenly matched. Let there be peace between us."

So it was. The chief never dared harm Aja or his brothers again. And when they finally did come to die, they all were transformed to wonderful things: okra and tomato, onion and eggplant. The fetish priest became pepper—but Aja, oh Aja became the king of the lot. He became hotter pepper and ruled them all.

Which Is the
Greatest Magician?

Three Magicians from the Ga of Ghana

One day, three magicians were strolling along when they came to a flooded river. All three wished to cross. But the water was very fierce and the river was very wide.

"We shall use our magic," the three decided. But each magician picked a different spell to use.

The first magician pulled out a thread and threw it across the river. It became a bridge, and he walked calmly across the river; then, he drew the thread back into his pouch.

"My magic is the strongest," he claimed.

The second magician took out his snuff bottle and called all the water into it. He walked calmly across the dry riverbed to the other side, then turned and called all the water back into the river where it belonged.

"*My* magic is the strongest," he claimed.

The third magician conjured up a fire that dried up all the water into great clouds of steam. He, too, walked calmly across the riverbed, then conjured away the fire so that the steam rained back down into the river again.

"*My* magic is the strongest," he claimed.

So now, here is the question. Think it over. Solve it as you see fit. For the answer is strictly your own and belongs only to you.

Which magician of the three is the greatest?

Notes

The folk motif numbers in this section refer to the exhaustive collection of the world's folk motifs made by Stith Thompson in his *Motif-Index of Folk Literature*. A folk motif is an element within a folktale that is a worldwide constant. For example, the magic lamp that appears in the tale of Aladdin is a folk motif.

Introduction

Shamanism can be found throughout the world, from the Inuit (who we misname as Eskimoes) to the peoples of the Amazonian jungles. Shamans can be of either gender, although most are male. Most shamanistic traditions involve the invoking of spirit helpers and visits of the shaman's own essense to the Other World, frequently through the use of drumming techniques and/or hallucinagens.

There are many books on shamanism, some better than others. The reader is advised to check both the authors' sources and credentials. One traditional source is *Shamanism*, by Mircea Eliade, listed in full in the Bibliography of this book.

The Lord of Pengerswick

This is the author's compilation of some of the several tales of the magical Lord of Pengerswick and his equally magical wife. Although not too many details are known about her, she is probably a Saracen, as medieval stories called the followers of Islam. There is nothing mysterious about the Witch of Fraddam; she is the typical medieval European witch who has sold her soul to the devil.

Readers familiar with the Greek story of Phaedra will notice a familiar motif: the wife who develops a passion for her stepson, is rebuffed by him, then makes a false claim of rape. In the story of Phaedra, this claim brings about the deaths both of her innocent son-in-law, Hippolytus, and herself. A less fatal version of the theme appears in the Old Testament story of Joseph, who narrowly escapes death when his master's wife falsely accuses him of assaulting her.

The sources for this tale include those gathered in the field by Robert Hunt, published in *Popular Romances of the West of England, or The Drolls, Traditions, and Superstitions of Old Cornwall*. Summaries are also included in Katherine Briggs' exhaustive compilation, *A Dictionary of British Folk-Tales*.

Motifs include A527.3. Culture hero as magician; D1711. Magician; D1719. Possession of magic powers; D1719.1 Contest in magic; D1738. Magic arts studied; G275.1. Witch carried off by devil; K2111. Potiphar's wife; S111. Murder by poisoning; T418. Lustful stepmother.

Gwydion

This is only part of the long and complex tale of Gwydion, whose adventures are chronicled in the *Mabinogion* (or, more properly *Mabinogi*), a compilation of Welsh tales first assembled and written down in the fourteenth century. But the stories, particularly the first four, the "four branches" that include Gwydion, are much older, and belong firmly to the world of folklore and myth. Arguments continue among scholars as to just how old the "four branches" may be: Elements in the tales make a good case for pre-Christian roots, which could date them as far back as the first millennium BCE.

Gwydion and his uncle Math, as well as other characters in the "four branches," have also been the center of debate. Some scholars claim that Gwydion and Math are "downgraded" deities, others that they were real men about whom fantastic tales grew, but no firm proof can be given for either claim.

The source of the story is of course the *Mabinogion*. The author used three translations, those of Jeffrey Gantz, Gwyn and Thomas Jones, and Patrick K. Ford.

Motifs include: D29. Transformation to a person of different social class—miscellaneous; D152.2. Transformation: man to eagle; D431.1 Transformation: flower to person; D451. Transformation of vegetable form; D1710. Possession of magic powers; D1711. Magician; D1711.11. Family of magicians; K2213.4.1. Secret of vulnerability disclosed by hero's wife; T540. Miraculous birth; T586.3. Multiple birth as result of relations with several men; T610. Nurture and growth of children; T670. Adoption of children; Z252. Hero at first nameless; Z310. Unique vulnerability.

Michael Scott

The real Michael Scott (1175-1234) was an astrologer and self-professed magician, a learned man of gentle birth who travelled all over Europe during his studies. Not too many details are known of his life. He may have served at the court of the Holy Roman Emperor Frederick II, probably authored the book on astrology attributed to him, as well as several other texts, and may even have taken holy orders.

Similar stories of a clever pupil escaping from the diabolical Black School have been told about other real men, mostly ministers in Scandinavia and Germany, such as Martin Luther, while the Black School turns up in tales from countries ranging from Norway through Spain.

Michael Scott is not the only magician to use the devil as a riding horse. The same tale is told of Martin Luther, and of the Reverend Petter Dass of Norway, who was said to have been a great magician as well as a cleric. The theme also appears in Rimsky-Korsakoff's opera, *Christmas Eve.*

This tale is the author's compilation of many different versions of Scott's life and adventures, including those in Spence's *An Encyclopaedia of Occultism,* an anonymous book of *Scottish Fairy Tales,* Richard Cavendish's *Legends of the World,* and Barbara Ker Wilson's *Scottish Folk-tales and Leg nds.*

Motifs include: B161.3. Wisdom from eating serpent; D102. Transformation: devil to animal; D1738. Magic arts studied; G303.9.5.4. Devil carries man through air as swift as wind (thought); G303.19. Devil takes the hindmost; H1021.1. Task: making a rope of sand; and S241.2. Devil is to have last one who leaves "black school." An example of how common tales of Michael Scott were in Great Britain is the following motif assigned to him: G303.9.2.5. Devil and Michael Scott carry tide an additional five miles up River Wansbeck.

Mongan

Mongan is the name of an actual prince of Ireland. He was son of Fiachna, King of the powerful Dal nAraidhe sept, or clan; Fiachna died in battle in 626 AD, unprotected, despite the tale, by any supernatural entities. The name "Mongan" means "the hairy one," and indicates that he probably was born with a full head of hair—a sure sign in Irish folklore of a seer or magician. There are several tales of his adventures, but it isn't until the eleventh century that he makes his appearance as a magician and son—not of Fiachna but of Manannan mac Lir.

The sources of this story include versions in *Myth, Legend & Romance: An Encyclopedia of the Irish Folk Tradition,* by Dr. Daithi O hOgain, who includes a discussion of the various developments in the story of Mongan from historic to fantastic figure, and *The Celtic Tradition,* by Caitlin Matthews.

Motifs include: A527.3. Culture hero as magician; A527.3.1. Culture hero can transform self; D25.2. Transformation into a cleric (monk); D.1711. Magician; D.1719. Possession of magic powers; F371. Human being raised in fairyland; and K1371.4. Lover in disguise abducts beloved.

Friar Roger Bacon

Roger Bacon (1214-1294) was a real man, born in Somerset, England. A true scholar and scientist, he studied at Oxford and wrote several scientific treatises. But, as happens far too often with learned folk, he was looked at with suspicion by his fellows, and was forced to flee to Paris, where he survived various charges of sorcery and had most of his work suppressed by the Church. In 1266 Bacon was finally allowed to return to Oxford but only to be thrown into prison for fourteen years as a heretical sorcerer. All his books were burned. Since he was already seen as a sorcerer, it was an easy jump for folks to make him the hero of a cycle of magical tales.

This story is the author's condensation and combination of some of the many tales about Friar Bacon, based on such sources as W. Carew Hazlitt's *National Tales and Legends* and Lewis Spence's *An Encyclopaedia of Occultism.* Also see Katherine Briggs's *A Dictionary of British Folk-tales.*

Motifs include: D1719.1. Contest in magic; D1738. Magic arts studied; D2031. Magic illusion; D2120. Magic transportation; K210. Devil cheated of his promised soul; N.845. Magician as helper.

Virgil

The Virgil of this story, which is the author's condensing of several tales of the magician's exploits, is none other than the first century Roman poet, author of, among other things, the *Aeneid.*

The real man was a courtier about whom not the slightest rumor of magical doings ever circulated during his lifetime. The tenuous connection between the magic of poetry and the magic of spells was made in southern Italy during the early Middle Ages, possibly as early as the tenth century, and from then through the sixteenth century, Virgil's name was "plugged in" to fantastic tales of a powerful Italian magician.

Sources for this story include the "Life of Virgilius" that appeared in English in about 1508, which is reprinted in W. Carew Hazlitt's *National Tales and Legends* and in Lewis Spence's *An Encyclopaedia of Occultism*. Summaries are included in Richard Cavendish's *Legends of the World* and Brendan Lehane's volume *Wizards and Witches* in *The Enchanted World* series.

Motifs include: D230. Transformation: man to stone; D700. Person disenchanted; D812. Magic object received from supernatural being; D830. Magic object acquired by trickery; D1266. Magic book; D1710. Possession of magic powers; D1711.2. Virgil as magician; D1738. Magic arts studied; D2031. Magic illusion; D2031.1.2. People swim in imaginary rising river; K717. Deception into bottle (vessel).

Csucksari

In Hungarian folklore, a *taltos* is a person of great magical abilities. Some of these abilities, such as the lack of a need for sleep, mark him as not really being human, though he is always human-born. A *taltos* is usually born with a full set of teeth (like the full head of hair in Ireland, a sure sign of magic), and his adventures usually involve shape-shifting into animal form or, as in this story, even into flame. This shape-shifting ability, together with the *taltos*'s gifts for reading nature and commanding birds and animals, suggests that the *taltos* has his origins in shamanism. More on the possible link between the taltos and the shaman can be found in *Hungarian and Vogul Mythology,* by Geza Roheim.

There are also *taltos* horses in Hungarian folklore, magical beasts that serve as helpers to heroes; they seem to hold a kinship to the Wonder Horses of Slavic folklore.

This folktale, with its central theme of placing the sun and moon in the sky and its odd series of encounters and battles, is unusual in that in all its retellings across Hungary and part of Roumania, it varies almost not at all in its details. This may be due to the relatively limited distribution of the story; it may also imply that the original story from which the folktale has evolved was of religious importance to the pre-Christian people who first told it. Other folktales, by contrast, vary wildly in their variations: the six hundred (at least) variations of "Cinderella" throughout the world are a prime example. Anyone interested in the usual wide spread of a folktale should look at Alan Dundes' *Cinderella: A Casebook.*

Even though this folktale in its entirety lacks wide distribution, the concept of placing the sun and/or moon in the sky is a common one in world folklore; it is particularly common in the Pacific Northwest of America, wherein it is usually Raven who is the hero. The theme of the dragon-man, in particular one who is married to a human (or at least human-seeming) woman, is common throughout Slavic countries.

The source of this story is one collected in 1948 in Garbolc, Hungary, by Laszlo Kovacs from a Gypsy, Sandor Farkas, and published in Linda Degh's *Folktales of Hungary*. Similar versions, as already noted, have been collected throughout Hungary and Roumania. See W. Henry Jones and Lewis L. Kropf's *The Folk-tales of the Magyars* and, for partial Roumanian versions, *Romanian Folk Tales*, translated by Ana Cartianu.

Motifs include: A531. Culture hero overcomes monsters; B11.11. Fight with dragon; D285. Transformation: man to fire; D1710. Possession of magic powers; D1810. Magic knowledge; L16. Victorious youngest son.

Eirik

The real Eirik, Eirik Magnusson, lived from about 1637 to 1716, and attended the Cathedral School at Skalholt, which was rumored to contain some magical books in its library. (This isn't impossible; the Vatican Library actually does contain some purported magic books.) Eirik was believed by his contemporaries and those who came after him to be a priest-magician who only used his magic for good.

This tale is the author's compiling of stories about Eirik. The sources include stories collected in Iceland in the nineteenth century. English translations can be found in several books edited by Jacqueline Simpson, including *Scandinavian Folktales, Icelandic Folktales and Legends,* and *Legends of Icelandic Magicians*.

Motifs include: D1266. Magic book; D1710. Possession of magic powers; D1738. Magic arts studied; F455.2.2. Trolls are usually ugly, hideous, big and strong; F455.3.6. Trolls go about by night; F455.6.6. Trolls carry off people; F455.6.6.1. Stolen woman saved from trolls' dance.

Vainamoinen

This tale, the author's condensation of part of the much larger epic that is the *Kalevala*, is an odd mix, part mythic creation tale, part shamanistic duel—with its reliance on the song magic of the Northern traditions of Scandinavia and Russia and its easy transformations—and part a very human study of brash youth against ancient wisdom. It takes some time for Joukahaimen to rouse Vainamoinen to anger—but once he does, the older wizard's anger is terrible and almost totally merciless, as befits a character who is, after all, someone left over from the creation of the world.

Vainamoinen, ancient yet heroic and very powerful, was surely an inspiration for the fantasy wizard Gandalf (who also isn't truly human) from J.R.R. Tolkien's epic, *The Lord Of The Rings;* Tolkien, a Professor of Philology at Oxford University, taught himself Finnish so that he could read the *Kalevala* in the original.

The hunt of young Joukahaimen for other magicians he can duel and defeat is a theme that remains with us in both American and Japanese popular culture: We're all familiar with the Western image of the cocky young gunfighter challenging—and getting defeated by—the older, world-weary champion, while in Japan, the image is of the younger swordfighter challenging—and getting defeated by—the older, equally world-weary samurai.

The source of this story is, as mentioned above, the *Kalevala,* which is a collection of epic Finnish story-songs put into chronological order by Elias Lonnrot, a doctor interested in his nation's past, who first published the *Kalevala* in the nineteenth century. The two translations used here are by W.K. Kirby and Francis Peabody Magoun, Jr. Those interested in more about Lonnrot and the mythic world behind his work are referred to *Kalevala Mythology,* by Juha Y. Pentikainen and translated by Ritva Poom.

Motifs include: A262. Planting the earth; A268.1.2. Origin of oak; A511.1. Birth of culture hero; A527.3. Culture hero as magician; A527.4. Culture hero as poet (musician); T540. Miraculous birth.

Mindia

Mindia is one of many folkloric heroes who magically learn the speech of birds and animals by tasting *tabu* blood or food. The Teutonic Sigurd or Siegfrid gains the same knowledge after tasting the blood of Fafnir, the dragon he's slain, while for the Irish Fionn Mac Cumhail, wisdom comes after accidentally tasting juice from the roasting Salmon of Knowledge; many other less memorable heroes in many other tales are similarly granted the power of understanding what the wild things say. In some stories, this magical gift must never be mentioned or the hero will die. And of course, the idea of forbidden fruit, fruit that will open one's eyes to equally forbidden knowledge, is familiar to the Judeo-Christian and Islamic world.

Mindia's tale is based on the summary in *Legends of the World*, by Richard Cavendish, and on tales in *The Golden Fleece: Tales from the Caucasus* and *Yes and No Stories*, by George and Helen Papashvily.

Motifs include: B161.3. Wisdom from eating serpent; B215.1 Bird language; B216. Knowledge of animal languages; D1815.2. Magic knowledge of language of animals; D1815.4. Magic knowledge of tree language; D2091. Magical attack against enemy; G303.9.5. The devil as an abductor.

King Solomon

This isn't the easiest story to place, since it is told in America as well as Israel, and is popular among the Jews of Eastern Europe. It has, as a compromise, been placed in the European section of this book, since most of the tellings came from Europe.

King Solomon's name has been associated with wisdom since the days of his reign, which date to the first millennium BCE. As happened with other wise and learned men, he quickly became the center of a cycle of folktales naming him as a mighty magician. This folk tradition, which has no basis in fact, became popular with both Jews and Arabs; in the Arab versions, King Solomon becomes master not of demons—which in Jewish folklore are more amoral beings than evil—but of all the Djinn, good and evil alike.

Folk tradition has added yet another element to this tradition. It has turned the six-pointed star, the *Mogen David* or *Star of David*, often used as a symbol of Judaism, into something magical, the Seal of Solomon. This is the arcane sign that seals the genie in the bottle in the famous tale from the *Arabian Nights*. The Seal of Solomon also appears as a powerful magical symbol in Christian folktales and medieval *grimoires*, or books of magic. The *grimoire* (known as the *Key of Solomon*) has been falsely attributed to King Solomon.

Benaiah, who was one of King Solomon's war leaders in the Old Testament, here plays the traditional folkloric role of the questing hero; quests for magical objects or beings appear in folklore the world over.

The seemingly inappropriate laughter or weeping of the demon Ashmodai is another common theme in folklore, turning up in tales from Wales to Eastern Europe, although usually it is a human man's supernatural wife who laughs or weeps, often provoking a blow that breaks their marriage vows.

This story is known to the author; versions can be found in collections of Jewish folklore such as Nathan Ausubel's *A Treasury of Jewish Folklore,* Penninah Schram's *Jewish Stories One Generation Tells Another,* and Pinhas Sadeh's *Jewish Folktales,* which also discusses the possible etymology of the name Ashmodai/Asmodeus.

Motifs include: B480. Helpful insects; D1711.1.1. Solomon as master of magicians; D1810.0.10. Magical knowledge (wisdom) of Solomon; H1172. Task: bringing an ogre to court; H1210.2. Quest assigned by king; H1320. Quest for marvelous objects or animals; H1331. Quest for remarkable animal; J191.1. Solomon as wise man.

Volka

This tale is based on a Russian *byliny,* or folk epic ballad, that dates at its latest to the sixteenth century, but parts of it may be several centuries earlier. Rus is the old name for Russia; the *bylina* of Volka as it has come down to us reflects the later date, confusing a lesser threat from Turkey or India (the attacker varies with the versions of the *bylina*) with the very real twelfth and thirteenth century threat from the Mongols and their Golden Horde.

Volka himself may be based in part on the historical Prince Oleg Sviatoslavich, who ruled a principality in the tenth century. But Volka's name and magical abilities probably relate to an ancient Russian word, *volkhv,* which refers to someone who is a pagan priest and beneficent sorcerer; his tale might have its roots in shamanism.

The source of this tale are both the author's own memory and translations of various versions of the *bylina,* such as the translations in Alexander Pronin's *Byliny* and E.M. Almedingen's *The Knights of the Golden Table.* George Vernadsky's *Kievan Russia* also provided a glimpse of the history behind the *bylina.*

Motifs include: A511.1. Birth of culture hero; A511.4.1. Miraculous growth of culture hero; A527.1. Culture hero precocious; A527.3. Culture hero as magician; A527.3.1. Culture hero can transform self; D630. Transformation and disenchantment at will; D641.2. Transformation to gain access to enemy's camp (fortress); D651.3. Transformation to destroy enemy's property; D651.5. Transformation to spy enemy's camp; D659.4. Transformation to act as helpful animal; D.1719. Possession of magic powers.

Meng Luling or Ma Liang

Here is an example of how retellings of tales may vary in details yet remain basically the same. People, unless they are trained to remember flawlessly (like the West African *griots* and the pre-Christian Celtic bards), forget story details and "plug in" elements of their own. An easy way to see the process in action is to watch the children's game of "Telephone," in which a brief story is passed from child to child; by the time the last child is reached, the story has changed in a good many details!

Magical paintings that come to life are more common in Asia, particularly China and India, than elsewhere, although the concept has been used to charming effect in Crockett Johnson's modern children's stories tracing the adventures of "Harold and the Purple Crayon." The Greek tale of Pygmalion and Galatea seems at first to be a close relative of this type of tale, since it features a sculpture of a woman that comes to life, but this transformation is the result of the sculptor's prayers, not his magic.

The story of Meng Luling/Ma Liang has been collected many times. Some of the translations to be found in English include translations from two anonymous Chinese collections, *Lady in the Picture*, which features the Meng Luling version, and *The Frog Rider*, which features the Ma Liang version.

Motifs in both tales include: D435.2.1. Picture comes to life; D.1711. Magician; D.1719. Possession of magic powers. For Tale Two only: D810. Magic object as a gift; D812. Magic object received from a supernatural being.

Teteke

Teteke's story shows definite feminist aspects. Teteke has survived an abusive marriage, manages to free herself of her husband's still-angry spirit, then declares that she—going against all Manchu principles—will live happily alone and unwed. Of course her talents would give her the freedom to make such a claim!

Yet another of the characteristic talents attributed to shamans is the gift of divination. See also "The Blind Fortune-teller" in this book. The epic tale of Teteke's adventures has been in the oral tradition of the Manchu and neighboring peoples for centuries, but it wasn't until the late nineteenth and early twentieth centuries that written versions were compiled, primarily by Russian scholars. Manchuria is, of course, no longer a separate entity but is part of northeastern China.

Although this tale may seem unique to the Manchu region, the format of the episodic quest is one popular in folktales around the world (and in much American fantasy fiction today). One of the most obvious examples of such an adventure can be found in Odysseus' struggles to get home, chronicled, of course, in the *Odyssey*. Another familiar element in the Manchu tale is that of the boatman who must be paid for ferry service across a river into the Underworld; though he's not at all related, the Manchu half-a-man does seem to be a cousin to the Greek Charon who ferries souls across the River Styx. And there is a parallel between Teteke's journey to the Underworld and that of the ancient Mesopotamian goddess Inanna, who made that perilous journey to bring back the soul of her dead love, Tammuz. Unlike Teteke, Inanna's efforts fail and she nearly loses her own life. For the entire tale of Inanna's descent, or at least as much of the tale as has survived, see Samuel Noah Kramer's *Sumerian Mythology*.

The author has retold the tale of Teteke from the longer and more complex Manchu folk epic generally called "The Tale of the Nisan Shaman." The original includes lengthy descriptions of the various realms of the dead and Buddhist rewards and punishments. The only available English translation of the complete text is that of Stephen Durrant, published in *The Tale of the Nisan Shamaness*, compiled by Margaret Nowak and Durrant, but there is also a Russian translation, *Nishan' Samani Bitkhe*, by Maria Petrovna Volkova. The rhyming, formulaic nonsense phrases beginning each of the shaman's chants were taken from the original Manchu text.

Motifs include: A672.1. Ferryman on river in lower world (Charon); D.1711. Magician; D.1719. Possession of magic powers; E121.7. Resuscitation by magician; F162.2 Rivers in other world; H1270. Quest to lower world; N810. Supernatural helpers; Q93.2. Reward for resuscitating dead.

Chitoku

Chitoku falls into the category of the Wise Old Man, the wizard who, though no longer young, can well take care of himself. He has cousins in such characters as the Finnish Vainamoinen, who appears elsewhere in this book, and the fictional Gandalf, the wizard hero who plays an important role in J.R.R. Tolkien's fantasy epic, *The Lord of the Rings*. The Wise Old Man often appears in folklore and fiction as the mentor of the young hero, such as Merlin to

Arthur or, in the movie *Star Wars*, Obi-wan ben Kenobi to Luke Skywalker. For more on this theme, see the author's *Once Upon a Galaxy*.

This story was originally written down in the *Konjaku monogatarischu*, the *Tales of Times Now Past*, a collection of traditional tales that probably dates to the eleventh or twelfth centuries CE; the tales are probably much older than the collection itself. While there is no comprehensive English translation of the collection, some of the tales, including this one, have been translated by Royall Tyler and included in his *Japanese Tales*, and by Fanny Hagin Mayer in her *Ancient Tales in Modern Japan* and her translation of *The Yanagita Kunio Guide to the Japanese Folk Tale*. Chitoku is not the only monk-diviner in Japanese folklore; there are also tales about a famous diviner known as Seimei.

Motifs include: A527.3. Culture hero as magician; D.1719. Possession of magic powers; Q212. Theft punished; R211.4 Escape from slavery (pirates).

The Blind Fortune-teller

Korea has a long tradition of magicians such as the shamanistic *mutangs*, who can, according to traditions still alive in some regions, speak with the dead. While *mutangs* are usually female, Korean fortune-tellers can be of either gender and, at least in folklore, are also said to possess truly magical abilities. It's not unusual in the Korean folk tradition for a blind man to become a fortune-teller.

The motif of the blind man who can "see" without eyes isn't found only in Korea. Some Japanese films feature a blind samurai, while American folk culture and popular entertainments are full of blind characters, from detectives to warriors, who have such sensitive senses of hearing, smell and touch that they seem almost magical.

The sources of this tale are a story collected from Zon Teg-Ha in 1936 in Onyang and published in *Folk Tales from Korea*, by Zong In-Sob, and an almost identical version published in *Korean Folk & Fairy Tales*, by Suzanne Crowder Han. The ending in the original is a little more ambiguous, implying either that the demons are satisfied with the fortune-teller's death or that their duel with him will continue in the Other World. The author has chosen the latter interpretation. Stories about *mutangs* can be found in *Korean Folk Tales: Imps, Ghosts, and Fairies*, by Im Bang and Yi Ryuk.

Motifs include: D1820. Magic sight and hearing; D2176. Exorcising by magic; E728. Evil spirit possesses person; E728.1. Evil spirit cast out of person.

Shee Yee

The Hmong, who have a long tradition of shamanism, are an ethnic minority who have been fighting extermination for centuries. Caught up in the Vietnam War, and allied with Western forces, many died during the war or in post-war purges by the Pathet Lao. Many wound up in refugee camps in Thailand; some 10,000 others have emigrated to the United States, where they are undergoing the difficult task of fitting into a new country while keeping their folk culture and arts alive.

This is the author's condensation of Shee Yee's episodic and somewhat repetitious adventures and battles against evil spirits. To American eyes, he's a little like a peacekeeping marshal of the Old West, albeit in his case with the help of magic powers. Though Shee Yee is portrayed as a deadly archer and swordsman, at times he seems more akin both to the clever Odysseus, he of the Trojan Horse trick, and to the true tricksters of folklore such as Coyote of North America.

Several traditional themes are turned on their figurative ears in this story. The bow that no one but the hero can draw is a common theme, turning up for example, in such stories as the *Ramayana* of India, wherein Rama is the hero, and the *Odyssey* of Greece, the story of Odysseus; in Shee Yee's tale, the evil spirit makes a mockery of the theme. The same is true of the pipe no one but the hero can smoke; see other examples in the stories of Glooscap and Spider Woman elsewhere in this book. But in Shee Yee's tale, once again the theme is turned upside down, with the evil spirit being the victor.

The sources of this tale are the lengthy folk epic collected from Pa Chou Yang, translated by Se Yang and Charles Johnson and published by Charles Johnson in *Myths, Legends and Folk Tales from the Hmong of Laos,* and the tales of Shee Yee collected by Jean Larteguy and Yang Dao in *Le Dragon, Le Maitre du Ciel et Ses Sept Filles* and by Jean Mottin in *Contes et Legends Hmong Blanc.* There is a related variant, as well as a brief cultural history, in *Folk Stories of the Hmong,* by Norma J. Livo and Dia Cha.

Motifs include: D12. Transformation: man to woman; D114.1.1. Transformation: man to deer; D180. Transformation: man to insect;

D283. Transformation: man to water; D671. Transformation flight; D1840. Magic invulnerability.

Djunban

The hill under which Djunban is said to be buried actually exists. Gold has been dug out of the hill, but no one has found any bodies.

The dramatic barrenness of the Australian outback, particularly of the Western Desert, makes it clear that a rainmaker such as Djunban would indeed be a powerful, valuable member of his community.

There are elements in this story that are unique to the Australian Aboriginals and don't "translate" well, such as the strange people carried under Djunban's skin. Are they spirit helpers? They never seem to serve that, or indeed any function. This ambiguity brings out a point about folklore: Folktales are often full of elements that don't seem to make sense. This can mean that these elements were so familiar to the original audience that they didn't need to be spelled out, but it can also mean that in the retelling from one generation to the next, someone accidentally left out some crucial bit of information. Either way, Djunban's basic function as a shamanistic rainmaker seems clear enough—as does the grief and guilt over his sister's death that leads to his own downfall.

The sources of this story, which the author has shortened from the episodic original, were two versions collected from George Maning and Tommy Nedabi of the Wirangu and Kukata language groups by R. Berndt in the Western Desert of Australia in 1941. They are included in *The Speaking Land* by Ronald M. Berndt and Catherine H. Berndt. Other tales of Aboriginal rainmakers can be found in *Australian Legendary Tales*, collected by K. Langloh Parker. A summary of various rainmaking rituals is included in the dictionary *Aboriginal Mythology*, by Mudrooroo.

Motifs include: D1028. Magic shell of animal; D1080. Magic weapons; D2143.1. Rain produced by magic; N330. Accidental killing or death.

Kukali

Kukali epitomizes the Polynesian love of exploring that took them across the Pacific to Samoa, Tahiti, Hawaii and other isolated islands. But he is also a familiar heroic type of many stories, both folk and media: the wandering loner who fights off monsters and human foes, rescues captives, and sometimes wins himself a mysterious wife. Great bird-demons such as Halulu are familiar figures in Polynesian folklore; they sometimes appear as shape-shifting sorcerers. Halulu as a bird is related to the Arabian Roc involved in the adventures of Sindbad the Sailor, and to other oversized birds in North American folklore. Humanity seems to like tales of ordinary creatures turned into giants. Fantasy novels often feature giant spiders, while campy movies such as *Rodan*, starring a Japanese prehistoric bird, remain popular.

The main source of this tale is one collected by William D. Westervelt, and is printed in his *Hawaiian Legends of Ghosts and Ghost-Gods*. However, he fails to include the informant's name or the date of collection. Other sources included variants found in Betty Allen's *Legends of Old Hawaii*—in which Kukali is a foundling who washes up on shore as a baby—and Erick Berry's *The Magic Banana and Other Polynesian Tales*.

Motifs include: C211. Tabu: eating in other world; D1711. Magician; F158. Pit entrance to otherworld; F813.6. Extraordinary banana; H1161.1. Killing murderous bird; R13.3. Bird carries off persons.

Tsak

This is the author's condensing of a longer and more episodic tale that includes more of Tsak's pre-shamanesque pranks and his winning a first wife—who is promptly forgotten. Tsak, a born survivor and optimist, is as much trickster as shaman, though the two categories aren't mutually exclusive. Although Tsak is unknown outside his culture, several elements in his story are known in tales throughout the world. Almost every culture has some variation on the "city in the clouds," the world in the sky that can only be reached by magic, such as by the famous beanstalk in "Jack and the Beanstalk." The magical bath, which is meant to boil the hero to death, turns up in many European tales, from Ireland to Russia. What is unusual in Tsak's tale is that only he enters the boiling bath. The usual form of this story has the hero magically surviving the bath and becoming magically handsome; the envious king leaps in, only to be boiled to death.

The mouse woman who aids Tsak is none other than Mouse Woman, a *narnauk* or animal-person, a powerful spirit being known to the Bella Coola and Haida peoples as well as to the Tsimshian. Mouse Woman is a grandmotherly figure who often aids humans. She hates disorder and disciplines trouble-makers, human or other. See the Hopi story of "Spider Woman" elsewhere in this book for a somewhat similar being.

The sources of this story are one recorded by William Beynon from Helen Clifton, Hartley Bay, British Columbia, in 1954, and printed in *Tsimshian Narratives I*, edited by John J. Cove and George F. MacDonald, and the tales collected in British Columbia by Franz Boas and published in his *Tsimshian Mythology* and *Tsimshian Texts*.

Motifs include: B450. Helpful birds; D810. Magic object a gift; D812.11. Magic object received from giant; D931. Magic rock (stone); D931.0.4. Magic stone as amulet; D1394. Magic object helps hero in trial; D1394.1. Trial by ordeal subverted by carrying magic object; D1470.1. Magic wishing-object; D1532.1. Magic flying skin; D1581. Task performed by use of magic object; F10. Journey to upper world; H931. Tasks assigned in order to get rid of hero; N810. Supernatural helpers.

Taligvak

The tale of Taligvak takes a practical look at magic: it's foolish to waste such a powerful tool when a job can done more easily by normal means! This tale also makes a societal point: It shows how people can be afraid of someone who isn't like them, and how they can cover fear with contempt—an all too common world motif.

Taligvak's song magic is typical of Inuit shamans—generally known among the Inuit peoples as *anatquqs*—and indeed of many others, including the Finnish Vainamoinen and the Manchu Teteke, whose tales appear in this book. The sources of this story were a tale collected and translated from the Copper Inuit people by Maurice Metayer and published in *Tales from the Igloo* (although no specific informant is singled out of the list of those who related tales) and a similar story collected by Diamond Jenness in the Mackenzie Delta of Canada and published in *Myths and Traditions from Northern Alaska, the Mackenzie Delta, and Coronation Gulf*; however, this second tale does not give the *anatquq* a name. Another useful collection of Inuit folklore, one including several stories of *anatquqs*, is *The Eskimo Storyteller*, collected by Edwin S. Hall, Jr.

Motifs include: D1710. Possession of magic powers; D1711. Magician; D2105. Provisions magically produced.

Spider Woman

Spider Woman, who can be either helpful or destructive depending on the situation and her wish, turns up as a benefactor in several Southwestern cultures. For example, while the Navajo and Hopi are two definitely different peoples, both include Spider Woman in their creation mythologies, and the Pawnee, who aren't related to either culture, call her Red Spider Woman or Witch Woman, and see her as a teacher of plant medicine.

Puukonhoya is actually a twin whose brother is named Palunhoya, and the two are heroic characters in several Hopi tales; in many of these tales, they are aided by Spider Woman. Hero twins are common in the folklore and mythology of North and South America, turning up in the tales of the Navajo, Seneca and Zuni as well as those of the Hopi.

The main sources of this tale are two versions, one recorded in *American Indian Myths and Legends,* edited by Richard Erdoes and Alfonso Ortiz, the other in *Spider Woman Stories,* by G.M. Mullett; versions can be found in other collections of Southwestern folklore, particularly Hopi, as well.

Motifs include: A527.3. Culture hero as magician; A527.3.1. Culture hero can transform self; B450. Helpful birds; H924.1. Tasks assigned as ransom; H982. Animals help man perform task; H1141. Task: eating enormous amount; H1511. Heat test. Attempt to kill hero by burning him in fire; H1562.1. Test of strength: pulling up tree by roots; N810. Supernatural helpers; R11.2. Princess (maiden) abducted by monster (ogre).

Asidenigan

Asidenigan is very much in the mold of the loner hero, the man who is more at home in the wilderness than in more civilized surroundings. Our American culture has a long tradition of such a figure, the outsider who knows the wilderness (whether natural wilderness or the cityscapes of the "film noire") with almost magical skill. He appears in Westerns, detective fiction and science fiction. He is the mysterious fellow who comes in from nowhere to set things right, who then disappears once more. Examples range from James Fennimore Cooper's literary creation, Hawkeye/Natty Bumpo, created in the mid-eighteenth century, to the mutant hero, the Mariner, in the 1995 science fiction movie, *Waterworld.*

The source of this story is, primarily one collected from James Mink through the interpreter Prosper Guibord by Ernestine Friedl in 1942 at the Lac Court Oreilles reservation in northern Wisconsin. It was printed in Victor Barnouw's *Wisconsin Chippewa Myths and Tales.* Furthermore, similar tales are collected in Henry Rowe Schoolcraft's collections of Chippewa lore, published in one volume as *Schoolcraft's Indian Legends.* Schoolcraft, working in the first half of the nineteenth century, was one of the first to see the value of collecting folk material from the indigenous tribes, particularly from the Chippewa, his wife's people.

Motifs include: D631.1. Person changes size at will; D1810.0.2. Magic knowledge of magician; D1980. Magical invisibility.

Glooscap

This is the author's combining of two traditional tales of Glooscap, which is intended to show something of this figure's fluid, mysterious nature. Glooscap certainly *is* a mysterious character, often spirit-like, if not an outright deity. However, the tales argue about this point. A giant, a magician, a creator (of humanity, some tales say) and even a trickster playing pranks for the sake of amusement all can be found in Glooscap stories. He is usually portrayed in human or giant form, though he could, as this story shows, shapeshift into animal forms as well.

There are many tales throughout the world trying to explain the origin of such pests as mosquitoes, which are often said, in Africa as well as North America, to have come from evil beings transformed into such nasty shapes so that they can continue to bother humanity.

The term "Wabanaki" refers to such related peoples as the Passamaquoddy, mostly of Maine, and the Micmac, mostly of Nova Scotia; both tribal groups tell very similar Glooscap tales. The specific sources are those collected by Charles G. Leland at the turn of the century and published in his *Algonquin Legends of New England,* although he doesn't specify informants for each tale, and those collected from Mrs. Constance Traynor by Howard Norman and published in his *Northern Tales.* Other references were *Stories from the Six Worlds: Micmac Legends,* by Ruth Holmes Whitehead and *Canadian Wonder Tales,* collected by Cyrus Macmillan.

Motifs include: A527.3 Culture hero as magician; A531. Culture hero (demigod) overcomes monsters; A527.3.1. Culture hero can transform self; A2034. Origin of mosquitoes; D40. Transformation to likeness of another person; D142. Transformation, man to cat; F531.1.9. Frost-giants.

Asin

Asin was a culture hero to several of the peoples of the Argentinean Gran Chaco, including the Toba and Pilaga—"was" because even in the 1930s, when tales like this one were collected, the Toba were becoming assimilated into the Spanish mainstream and forgetting their folkloric heritage. By now, it's unlikely that Asin's adventures are recalled as more than an occasional story or a footnote in scholarly works. Asin was always a mysterious character, sometimes a hero along the lines of the more traditional human magician of folklore, sometimes a hero on the grander, more mythic scale, as one who introduced cultural elements such as clothes and tools to the region.

This tale contains elements from the male variant of the "Cinderella" story, sometimes referred to as "Cinderlad," the apparently ugly, worthless boy who is actually a hero in disguise. "Cinderlad" heroes in their ugly guises often trail after war parties, only to reveal themselves in their full heroic splendor during battle.

The sources of this tale are from several stories of Asin collected in the field by Alfred Metraux from Toba informants. They can be found in Metraux's *Myths of the Toba and Pilaga Indians of the Gran Chaco* (1933). Also, see the collection made by Raphael Karsten, *Indian Tribes of the Argentine and Bolivian Chaco*.

Motifs include: A527.3. Culture hero as magician; A527.3.1. Culture hero can transform self; A527.3.1.1. Culture hero assumes ugly and deformed guise; D1710. Possession of magic powers.

Setna and Se-Osiris

Setna actually existed. His real name was Khaemwaset, and he was the fourth son of Pharaoh Ramses II (ca. 1279-1213 BCE). Khaemwaset apparently wasn't interested in royal politics; his studies took him instead toward the Egyptian priesthood, wherein he became a High Priest. Then, as now, educated people were thought to have studied magic as well, and a cycle of tales sprang up about Khaemwaset's name, claiming that he had been a great magician. By the time this particular tale was written down, in the shorthand form of hieroglyphics known as demotic script, somewhere between the seventh and second centuries BCE, Khaemwaset's true name had been forgotten and replaced with Setna, which is probably derived from the ancient Egyptian word *set'n*, or priest. Egyptian priests were permitted to marry, but we don't know whether the historic Khaemwaset had a son.

There was a long-standing political feud between Egypt and its neighbor to the south, then known as Nubia, now parts of the Sudan and Ethiopia. Although spells probably were attempted by both sides, there's no evidence of any magical duels.

This tale is a somewhat condensed version of such translations of the demotic text as that given by Gaston Maspero in his *Popular Stories of Ancient Egypt* and F.L. Griffith in *Stories of the High Priests of Memphis*. The author has taken the liberty of making it Setna—who is, after all, the older and more experienced magician—rather than his young son who successfully defeats the Nubian magician in sorcerous combat. Another source of information about Khaemwaset, which provides a picture of his statue and a photograph of one of the original demotic papyri about him as a magician, is *Magic in Ancient Egypt*, by Geraldine Pinch. The curious will also find a photograph of a portrait statue of Khaemwaset in the same book; according to this statue, he was, as the author has portrayed him, tall and handsome.

Motifs include: D418.1. Serpent (snake) to other animal; D908. Magical darkness; D1271. Magic fire; D1402.4. Magic fire kills; D1711. Magician; D1737. Magical power inherited; D1825.4. Ability to see hidden things; F695. Extraordinary reading ability.

Mbokothe

This story is a variation of a tale type known throughout the world as "The Magician and his Pupil." In its full form, the basic story tells of a boy apprenticed to a magician. The boy learns shape-shifting, has himself sold at market in animal form to benefit his poor parents or siblings, then is caught by the magician. A magicians' duel of shape-shifting follows, ending in the apprentice killing the magician. In the story of Mbokothe, the basic tale has been reduced to the most basic elements, and lacks the finality of one combatant's death. Instead, Mbokothe is taught a valuable lesson about not misusing power.

The source of this tale is one collected in *Akamba Stories*, collected by John S. Mbiti, and in *African Folktales* by Roger D. Abrahams.

Motifs include: D100. Transformation: man to animal; D610. Repeated transformation; D612. Protean sale; man sells youth in successive transformations; D671. Transformation flight; D1721. Magic power learned from magician; K252. Selling one's self and escaping.

Elephant Girl

Elephant Girl is a strange being, indeed. Although she has been born into a human society and seems to be a part of that society, she also has unspecified but definite ties to the animal world as well. Was she originally an elephant spirit or a shape-shifter? Odd hints of a dual nature turn up in a British "Cinderella" variant, "Cat Skin," as well. In "Cat Skin" the heroine wears a catskin disguise yet shows signs, such as twitching her ears, that she may originally have shape-shifted into cat shape.

Precocious babies, born able to speak and otherwise act like older children, are usually hero figures in folklore. See, for example, the tale of "Volka" in this book. The precocious baby in Elephant Girl's story, however, is definitely evil, an ancestor, perhaps, of all those "demon baby" books and movies so beloved of modern horror fiction fans.

Miraculous returns to life, whether to mortal life or to another form of existence altogether are, not surprisingly, common to all the world's folklore and mythology. For another example of this widespread theme, see the Welsh story of "Gwydion."

The sources of this story are two versions collected by Megan Biesele, the first from !Unn/obe N!a'an, Kauri, Botswana, in 1972, the second from //Xukxa N!a'an, Dobe, Botswana in 1971, and printed in her *Women Like Meat: The Folklore and Foraging Ideology of the Kalahari Ju/'Hoan.*

Motifs include A527.3. Culture hero as magician; D1011.1. Magic animal horn; E32.0.1. Eaten person resuscitated; E50. Resuscitation by magic; E113. Resuscitation by blood; E232.1. Return from the dead to slay own murderer; G10. Cannibalism.

Clever Aja

Aja, like the Hungarian *taltos* magician Csucskari, is a youngest son. (And, as every child knows, it's almost always the youngest son who triumphs in a folktale.) In Aja's case, a magical element is added: he is the seventh son. Although such elements in this story, such as magic being worked with a cowtail switch and as the transformation of the characters after their deaths into plant form, are specifically West African, the idea of the seventh son or daughter—or sometimes the seventh son of a seventh son—being magical is found in the stories of countries the world over. Seven, along with three, six and nine, is generally considered a magical number.

Young men or women sent on seemingly impossible quests by cruel rulers turn up in tales from China to the Americas, and inanimate objects or animals who help the protagonist because he or she has been kind to them are just as common.

Death often turns up as a personified figure in world folklore. Sometimes he (rarely she) appears as an antagonist to be fought, outwitted, or captured—in the latter case, only to be released again since a world without the relief of death turns out to be intolerable. But sometimes Death appears as a more beneficent figure, sometimes serving, in a theme familiar throughout Europe and part of Asia, as the hero's godfather; these tales, through no fault of Death's own, usually end with the hero's demise. (The idea of a personified Death carries over into modern drama and fiction, such as the successful play and movie, *Death Takes a Holiday* and the rather likeable figure in many of fantasy author Terry Pratchett's Diskworld novels.)

The sources of this story are a tale collected in the field by Jack Berry in the 1950s and published in *West African Folk Tales,* edited by Richard Spears, and one collected in R.K. Rattray's *Akan-Ashanti Folk-tales.*

Motifs include: A2610. Creation of plants by transformation; D672. Obstacle flight; E50. Resuscitation by magic; E53. Resuscitation by fetish; H1211. Quests assigned in order to get rid of hero; H1210.2. Quest assigned by king; H1235.1. Helpers on quest demand pay for advice; L50. Victorious younger brother; T586.1.2. Seven children at a birth; Z111. Death personified.

Which Is the Greatest Magician?

This is the type of puzzle story popular in many cultures, from Africa to Asia to America: the riddle that has no end. While children often use puzzle stories as "gotchas," a triumph of the teller over the listener, in tales told by adults to adults around the world, this type of story is meant to rouse the listener to—hopefully logical—thought, without ever resolving anything with a definite right answer. Since magic is such a mysterious thing, and magicians, since they work with this nebulous force, are puzzling as well, it seems only fitting to end this book with an unresolved tale.

The main source of this story is a tale collected in Ghana by Jack Berry in the 1950s and recorded in his *West African Folk Tales;* however, similar versions can be found in such collections as

African Folktales by Paul Radin, and *African Folklore,* collected by Richard M. Dorson.

Motifs include: D1710. Possession of magic powers; D2140. Magical control of elements.

Bibliography

Abrahams, Roger D. *African Folktales*. New York: Pantheon Books, 1983.

Aldinton, Richard and Delano Ames, trans. *Larousse Encyclopedia of Mythology*. London: Paul Hamlyn, 1959.

Allen, Betty. *Legends of Old Hawaii*. Honolulu: Tongg Publishing Company, 1955.

Almedingen, E.M. *The Knights of the Golden Table*. Philadelphia: J.P. Lippincott, 1964.

Anonymous, ed. *The Frog Rider: Folktales from China*. Beijing: Foreign Languages Press, 1957.

Anonymous, ed. *Lady in the Picture: Chinese Folklore*. Beijing: Chinese Literature Press, 1993.

Anonymous, ed. *Scottish Fairy Tales*. London: Bracken Books, 1993.

Anonymous, ed. *The Secret Arts: A Volume of the Enchanted World*. Alexandria, Virginia: Time-Life Books, 1987.

Ausubel, Nathan. *A Treasury of Jewish Folklore*. New York: Crown Publishers, 1948.

Barnouw, Victor. *Wisconsin Chippewa Myths & Tales and Their Relation to Chippewa Life*. Madison: The University of Wisconsin Press, 1977.

Berndt, Ronald M. and Catherine H. Berndt. *The Speaking Land: Myth and Story in Aboriginal Australia*. Victoria, Australia: Penguin Books, 1989.

Berry, Erick. *The Magic Banana and Other Polynesian Tales*. New York: The John Day Company, 1968.

Berry, Jack. *West African Folk Tales*. Evanston, Illinois: Northwestern University Press, 1991.

Biesele, Megan. *Women Like Meat: The Folklore and Foraging Ideology of the Kalahari Ju/'Hoan*. Bloomington: Indiana University Press, 1993.

Boas, Franz. *Tsimshian Mythology*. Washington: Government Printing Office, 1916.

———. *Tsimshian Texts, New Series*. Leiden and New York: Publications of the American Ethnological Society, Vol. III, 1912.

Briggs, Katherine M. *A Dictionary of British Folk-tales*. Vol. 2, *Local Legends*. Bloomington: Indiana University Press, 1971.

Butler, E.M. *The Myth of the Magus*. Cambridge: Cambridge University Press, 1948.

Calvino, Italo. *Italian Folktales*. New York: Harcourt Brace Jovanovich, 1980.

Cartianu, Ana, trans. *Romanian Folk Tales*. Bucharest: Editura Minerva, 1979.

Cavendish, Richard, ed. *Legends of the World*. New York: Schocken Books, n.d.

Cove, John J. and George F. MacDonald, eds. *Tsimshian Narratives I: Tricksters, Shamans and Heroes*. Ottawa: Canadian Museum of Civilization, 1987.

Degh, Linda, ed. *Folktales of Hungary*. Translated by Judit Halasz. Chicago: University of Chicago Press, 1965.

Dorson, Richard M. *African Folklore*. New York: Anchor Books, 1972.

————. *Folktales Told Around the World*. Chicago: University of Chicago Press, 1975.

Dundes, Alan. *Cinderella: A Casebook*. Madison: The University of Wisconsin Press, 1982.

Eberhard, Wolfram, ed. *Folktales of China*. Chicago: University of Chicago Press, 1965.

Eliade, Mircea. *Shamanism: Archaic Techniques of Ecstasy*. Translated by Willard R. Trask. Princeton: Princeton University Press, 1964.

Erdoes, Richard and Alfonso Ortiz, eds. *American Indian Myths and Legends*. New York: Pantheon Books, 1984.

Ford, Patrick, trans. and ed. *The Mabinogi and Other Medieval Welsh Tales*. Berkeley: University of California Press, 1977.

Gantz, Jeffrey, trans. and ed. *The Mabinogion*. Harmondsworth, Middlesex: Penguin Books Ltd., 1976.

Gill, Sam D. and Irene F. Sullivan. *Dictionary of Native American Mythology*. Santa Barbara: ABC-CLIO Inc., 1992.

Green, Roger Lancelyn. *A Book of Magicians*. New York: Puffin Books, 1977.

Griffith, F.L. *Stories of the High Priests of Memphis*. Oxford: Oxford University Press, 1900.

Hall, Edwin S., Jr., ed. *The Eskimo Storyteller: Folktales from Noatak, Alaska*. Knoxville: The University of Tennessee Press, 1975.

Han, Suzanne Crowder. *Korean Folk & Fairy Tales*. Seoul: Hollym International Corporation, 1991.

Hazlitt, W. Carew. *National Tales and Legends or Tales and Legends of National Origin or Widely Current in England from Early Times*. London: Swan Sonnenshein, 1892.

Hubbs, Joanna. *Mother Russia.* Bloomington: Indiana University Press, 1988.

Hunt, Robert. *Popular Romances of the West of England or The Drolls, Traditions, and Superstitions of Old Cornwall.* New York: Benjamin Blom, 1916.

Im Bang and Yi Ryuk, *Korean Folk Tales: Imps, Ghosts, and Fairies.* Translated by James S. Gale. Rutland, Vermont: Charles E. Tuttle Company, 1962.

Ivanits, Linda J. *Russian Folk Belief.* Armonk, New York: M.E. Sharpe, Inc., 1989.

Jenness, Diamond. *Myths and Traditions from Northern Alaska, the Mackenzie Delta, and Coronation Gulf.* Vol. 13A *Report of the Canadian Arctic Expedition 1913-18.* Ottawa: F.A. Acland, 1924.

Johnson, Charles, trans. and ed. *Myths, Legends and Folk Tales from the Hmong of Laos.* St. Paul: Macalaster College, 1985.

Johnson, Crockett. *Harold and the Purple Crayon.* New York: Harper & Row, 1955.

Jones, Gwyn and Thomas Jones, trans. and eds. *The Mabinogion.* London: J. M. Dent & Sons, 1949.

Jones, W. Henry and Lewis L. Kropf. *The Folk-tales of the Magyars.* London: Publications of the Folk-lore Society, 1889.

Karsten, Raphael. *Indian Tribes of the Argentine and Bolivian Chaco.* Helsinfors: Societas Scientiarum Fennica 4:1, 1932.

Kramer, Samuel Noah. *Sumerian Mythology.* New York: Harper & Brothers, 1961.

Kvideland, Reimund and Henning K. Sehmsdorf, eds. *Scandinavian Folk Belief and Legend.* Minneapolis: University of Minnesota Press, 1988.

Larteguy, Jean and Yang Dao. *Le Dragon, Le Maitre du Ciel et Ses Sept Filles.* Paris: Editions G.P., 1978.

Lehane, Brendan. *Wizards and Witches: A Volume of the Enchanted World.* Alexandria, Virginia: Time-Life Books, 1984.

Leland, Charles G. *The Algonquin Legends of New England.* Boston: Houghton Mifflin, 1884.

Livo, Norma J. and Dia Cha. *Folk Stories of the Hmong.* Englewood, Colorado: Libraries Unlimited, 1991.

Lonnrot, Elias, comp. *Kalevala.* Translated by W.F. Kirby. London: J. M. Dent & Sons, 1907.

———. *The Kalevala.* Translated by Francis Peabody Magoun, Jr. Cambridge, Massachusetts: Harvard University Press, 1963.

Macmillan, Cyrus. *Canadian Wonder Tales.* Toronto: The Bodley Head, 1974.

Maspero, Gaston. *Popular Stories of Ancient Egypt.* Translated by A. S. Johns. New Hyde Park, New York: University Books, 1967.

Matthews, Caitlin. *The Celtic Tradition.* Shaftsbury, Dorset: Element Books, 1995.

Mayer, Fanny Haagin, ed. and trans. *Ancient Tales in Modern Japan: An Anthology of Japanese Folk Tales.* Bloomington: Indiana University Press, 1948.

————. *The Yanagita Kunio Guide to the Japanese Folk Tale.* Bloomington: Indiana University Press, 1948.

Mbiti, John S. *Akamba Stories.* Oxford: Oxford University Press, 1966.

Metayer, Maurice. *Tales from the Igloo.* Edmonton, Alberta: Hurtig Publishers, 1972.

Metraux, Alfred. *Myths of the Toba and Pilaga Indians of the Gran Chaco.* Philadephia: American Folklore Society, 1946.

Mottin, Jean. *Contes et Legendes Hmong Blanc.* Bangkok: Don Bosco Press, 1980.

Mudrooroo. *Aboriginal Mythology.* London: HarperCollins Publishers, 1994.

Mullett, G.M. *Spider Woman Stories: Legends of the Hopi Indians.* Tucson: The University of Arizona Press, 1979.

Norman, Howard. *Northern Tales: Traditional Stories of Eskimo and Indian Peoples.* New York: Pantheon Books, 1990.

Nowak, Margaret and Stephen Durrant. *The Tale of the Nisan Shamaness: A Manchu Folk Epic.* Seattle: University of Washington Press, 1977.

O hOgain, Dr. Daithi. *Myth, Legend & Romance: An Encyclopedia of the Irish Folk Tradition.* New York: Prentice Hall Press, 1991.

Papashvily, George and Helen. *Yes and No Stories: A Book of Georgian Folk Tales.* New York: Harper and Brothers, 1946.

Parker, K. Langloh. *Australian Legendary Tales.* Sydney: Angus and Robertson, 1953.

Pentikainen, Juha Y. *Kalevala Mythology.* Translated by Ritva Poom. Bloomington: Indiana University Press, 1989.

Pinch, Geraldine. *Magic in Ancient Egypt.* Austin: University of Texas Press, 1994.

Pronin, Alexander. *Byliny: Heroic Tales of Old Russia.* Frankfurt: Possev-Verlag, 1971.

Pyman, Avril, trans. *The Golden Fleece: Tales from the Caucasus.* Moscow: Progress Publishers, 1971.

Radin, Paul. *African Folktales.* New York: Princeton University Press, 1962.

Rattray, R.S. *Akan-Ashanti Folk-tales.* Oxford: Oxford University Press, 1930.

Riordan, James. *The Sun Maiden and the Crescent Moon: Siberian Folk Tales.* New York: Interlink Books, 1989.

Roheim, Geza. *Hungarian and Vogul Mythology.* Vol. 23. *Monographs of the American Ethnological Society.* Locust Valley, New York: J.J. Augustin Publisher, 1954.

Sadeh, Pinhas. *Jewish Folktales.* New York: Anchor Books, 1989.

Schoolcraft, Henry Rowe. Mentor L. Williams, editor. *Schoolcraft's Indian Legends.* East Lansing: Michigan State University Press, 1991.

Schram, Peninnah. *Jewish Stories One Generation Tells Another.* Northvale, New Jersey: Jason Aronson Inc., 1987.

Sherman, Josepha. *Once Upon a Galaxy.* Little Rock: August House, Inc., 1994.

Simpson, Jacqueline, trans. and ed. *Legends of Icelandic Magicians.* Cambridge: D.S. Brewer Ltd. and Rowman & Littlefield, 1975.

———. *Icelandic Folktales and Legends.* Berkeley: University of California Press, 1972.

———. *Scandinavian Folktales.* New York: Penguin Books, 1988.

Spence, Lewis. *An Encyclopaedia of Occultism.* New Hyde Park, New York: University Books, 1960.

Thompson, Stith. *Motif Index of Folk Literature.* 6 vols. Bloomington: Indiana University Press, n.d.

Tyler, Royall. *Japanese Tales.* New York: Pantheon Books, 1987.

Vernadsky, George. *Kievan Russia.* New Haven: Yale University Press, 1948.

Volklova, Maria Petrovna. *Nishan' Samand Bitkhe.* Moscow: Akademia Nauk SSSR, Institut Narodov Azii, 1963.

Westervelt, William D. *Hawaiian Legends of Ghosts and Ghost-Gods.* Tokyo: Charles E. Tuttle Company, 1963.

Whitehead, Ruth Holmes. *Stories from the Six Worlds: Micmac Legends.* Halifax, Nova Scotia: Nimbus Publishing, Ltd., 1988.

Wilson, Barbara Ker. *Scottish Folk-tales and Legends.* London: Oxford University Press, 1954.

Zheleznova, Irina, ed. and trans. *A Mountain of Gems: Fairy-Tales from the People of the Soviet Union.* Moscow: Foreign Languages Press, 1963.

———. *Tales of the Amber Sea.* Moscow: Progress Publishers, 1974.

Zong, In-Sob. *Folk Tales from Korea.* Seoul: Hollym International Corporation, 1979.